DONATED BY

Friends of
Gale Free Library

HOLDEN,
MASSACHUSETTS

MACK McGINN'S Big Win

Also by Coleen Murtagh Paratore

THE WEDDING PLANNER'S DAUGHTER

THE CUPID CHRONICLES

26 BIG THINGS SMALL HANDS DO

HOW PRUDENCE PROOVIT PROVED THE
TRUTH ABOUT FAIRY TALES

MACK McGINN'S
Big Win

COLEEN MURTAGH PARATORE

Simon & Schuster Books for Young Readers
New York   London   Toronto   Sydney

SIMON & SCHUSTER BOOKS FOR YOUNG READERS
An imprint of Simon & Schuster Children's Publishing Division
1230 Avenue of the Americas, New York, New York 10020

SIMON & SCHUSTER BOOKS FOR YOUNG READERS is a trademark of
Simon & Schuster, Inc.
Book design by Lucy Ruth Cummins
The text for this book is set in Alinea Roman.
Manufactured in the United States of America
2 4 6 8 10 9 7 5 3 1
Library of Congress Cataloging-in-Publication Data
Paratore, Coleen, 1958–
Mack McGinn's big win / Coleen Paratore.—1st ed.
p. cm.
Summary: Whether the prize is a soccer trophy or the esteem of Danville's
elite, the McGinn family believes in winning, but while striving to prove he
can be best at something, sixth-grader Mack inadvertently demonstrates to
his parents and older brother what really matters most.
ISBN-13: 978-1-4169-1613-0
ISBN-10: 1-4169-1613-X
[1. Sports—Fiction. 2. Competition (Psychology)—Fiction. 3. Social classes—
Fiction. 4. Brothers—Fiction. 5. Family life—New York (State)—Fiction.
6. New York (State)—Fiction.]
I. Title.
PZ7.P2137Mac 2007
[Fic]—dc22
2006021959

WITH LOVE TO MY SONS—
CHRIS, CONNOR, AND DYLAN.
I SURE WON BIG WITH YOU.

—C. M. P.

CONTENTS

CHAPTER 1
MACK 'N' CHEESE

Q. WHY WAS CINDERELLA SO BAD AT SPORTS?
A. HER COACH WAS A PUMPKIN AND SHE RAN FROM THE BALL.

Winning runs in the family.

First turn, front seat, favorite show, fattest slice. Best stash of cash on your birthday.

But those are just the scrimmages. With me and Rory, the real thing is sports.

Our grandfather was "Red" McGinn, famous quarterback for the Fightin' Irish of Notre Dame. Here in Danville, there's a street, a school, a stadium, and an ice cream named for Gramp. There's a statue of him in the park.

"You're the spittin' image of him, Mack," people say to me. "The red hair, the freckles . . ." They shake their heads, sniffling. "Your grandfather was a hero, a legend."

I feel a punch in my gut when they say that. I miss Gramp so much.

My grandfather may have been the famous McGinn, but, like I said, winning runs in the family. My dad was a superstar soccer player, nearly made it to the Olympics. He had Rory and me dribbling soccer balls before we could walk.

What do McGinns do?

McGinns win!

How do McGinns win?

Anyway we can!

Dad doesn't play soccer anymore. He's a superstar salesman now.

Mom was a nationally ranked swimmer in college. Now she swims with the sharks selling Blue Ribbon real estate.

Bigger, better, best.

Never settle less.

Till your house is bigger.

Bigger, better, best!

We keep moving to new houses. We're moving to the "dream house" next month. I liked our first house, and we've only been in this second one a year, but nobody asked my opinion. I've got too much else to think about anyway. This is going to be a big year for me. The year I beat my big brother.

Beating Rory won't be easy. Rory never met a ball he didn't like. If a spaceship landed in Danville Park today and some weird, purple bobble-head creatures slithered out and started playing some whacked-out game, Rory would watch for about three seconds, shout "Count me in," and then beat the purple people at their own game. The bobble-heads would probably kidnap him back to their planet to be their new head coach.

All the coaches watch Rory. "That boy's going places," they say.

I remember when I was, like, three and Rory was five, my eyes were always blinking from all the cameras flashing after all of Rory's wins.

"Say cheese, Rory," Dad would say, all happy and proud.

"Cheese!" Rory would shout, waving a trophy in the air.

"Say cheese," Mom would gush, all happy and proud.

"Cheese!" Rory would scream, swinging a gold medal like a cowboy rope.

"*Cheese, cheese, cheese!*" I would shout, bouncing up and down, all excited. They were calling my favorite food. Those little white noodles, that cheesy sauce. "Macky, macky, macky," I'd say, shaking macaroni boxes like maracas in my hands.

I begged for "macky" in the morning, "macky" noon and night. That's how Rory named me. My real name is Matthew. In the family albums, there I am with that stupid orange grin, shoveling fistfuls of macaroni into my mouth.

One time, Rory thought it would be funny to stick macaroni in my other orifices too. Use *orifice* in a paper and I guarantee some teacher will be impressed. You owe me five bucks if you get an A. Anyway, there I was, eating my "macky," happier than a pig in poop, and Rory waited until Mom wasn't looking and then he stuck macaroni in my ear holes and up my nostrils, too. Way, far up.

I started crying, probably because I couldn't dig those noodles out to eat, and eventually they figured out the problem and rushed me to the emergency room. "Come on, Mackie, blow your nose," Mom kept pleading. "Come on, honey, *blow!*"

The doctor shoveled out my ears okay, but they had to suction my nose with a pump. That hurt. Poser Rory was crying, hugging me. "You're okay, little buddy, you're okay." He didn't even get in any trouble. *So lucky.* Trouble slides off Rory like butter off pancakes.

It's not that I'm not good. *I am.* Soccer, basketball—you should see me on a tennis court. The thing is, Rory's older. He burst out of my mother two years before me. Rory was *first.* And no matter what I do, there's no beating that. Everything I do, Rory's already done. Every game I win, Rory's already won.

I think when you're the first kid born in a family, before you leave the hospital, a nurse gives you a shot of luck in your butt, and after that, you're golden. No matter how old you get, or mean, or how badly you screw up, you will always be lucky.

I have a secret. At Camp Nassau this summer, I discovered something. It's not a new talent. I've always been good at it, but now I'm really, really good. Kids' eyes were bugging out and all the counselors made a big deal. Rory was at soccer camp. None of my friends were there. Mom and Dad weren't either.

That win was mine. No coaching, no cameras, no pressure. *Sweet*. It felt so sweet, I almost cried. I knew right then. I'd found my sport.

Just wait until Dad sees.

I start Danville Middle School tomorrow, sixth grade. Rory's in eighth. Next year, Rory might go to this high school in Florida where all the best soccer players go. Kids who have their pick of colleges. Kids who have a shot at the Olympics. I'm afraid Dad might move there with him. It's now or never for me.

I'm going to be sleek about this, though. If Rory gets even a hint of a clue, he'll start practicing and plotting and figure out some way to beat me. I'm going to keep Rory in the dark as long as I can, until I'm ready to make my move. Then, when I do, I'll beat him so badly, he'll wonder how he never saw it coming.

Trust me: This isn't going to be pleasant. My brother's been king for a very long time. King Rory the First won't relinquish his throne without a fight.

Relinquish is another fiver word. If you use it, you owe me.

The thing is, McGinns are winners. It's what everyone expects. Nobody notices normal wins anymore. It's going to take a big win, a really big win, to get some respect around here.

Don't get me wrong. There are some advantages to being the baby in the family. I figure you should milk the whole Santa Claus–Easter Bunny–Tooth Fairy deal as long as you can. Presents-candy-money? That's a no-brainer, right?

But with sports, I'm no pee-wee anymore.

This year, Mack's moving to the majors.

This year I'll be Mack Mc*Win*.

This year, finally, I will make my father proud.

CHAPTER 2
FIRST DAY

KINDERGARTEN TEACHER: WHO CAN NAME THE FOUR SEASONS?
LITTLE KID: I CAN! FOOTBALL, BASKETBALL, BASEBALL, HOCKEY.

Rory and Dad are eating breakfast, the sports section spread out between them. Buddy woofs hello and then slop-flops back to sleep. Bud's a big old golden retriever with a big goofy tail. It sweeps the ground like a fur mop when he walks. It's too bad that tail can't mop up the mud Bud drags into the house or wipe up the drool pools he leaves all over. Mom's just about had it with Bud. I think she wants to trade him in for a smaller, sleeker pooch, one of those skinny hotdogs with a foofy name and pointy ears.

"Morning, champ," Dad says. He slides me the juice, the cereal, and the bucket of bubblegum vitamin balls. "Big day, huh?"

Dad doesn't mean my first day at "DMS," Danville Middle School. Dad means the soccer tryouts afterward. Sometimes a few really good sixth graders make the team.

DMS is huge, sixteen hundred kids. Tons of seventh and eighth graders try out. Loads of kids get cut. Only one or two sixth graders ever make it. Rory did.

"Yeah, Dad." I look for green in the bucket. There's only pink and purple left. Rory got the last green one. He crinkles the wrapper to make sure I see.

"Be aggressive," Dad says. "Hit that field like a Mack truck. Get in that coach's face. And make sure he knows you're Rory's brother."

Rory sniffs. "That doesn't mean anything, Dad. Sixth graders hardly ever . . ."

Clickety clack, clickety clack. We hear Mom's heels before we see her. She rounds the bend like a train, *choo-choo*, newspapers swooshing up in the breeze. Buddy stands at attention, shrugs off the drool, and *woofs* a respectful salute. Bud knows he's just one slime soup away from the pound.

"Jeannie," Dad says, annoyed, "promise me when we move to Avalon, no high heels on the hardwood floors. They're Chilean inlaid parquet and they cost . . ."

"Chill, Bill," Mom says. "I don't shed my shoes for lumber. I don't care if it's Chilean inlaid gold." My mother loves fancy shoes. She's got about a hundred pairs.

"Speed it up, guys," Mom says. She has no patience for turtles.

Rory and I go upstairs and run the water to fake brushing our teeth.

General Mom is waiting by the door for inspections. "Sleep

bug, Mack. And a milk mustache." She brushes my shoulder. She looks down. "And zip the . . ."

"Lamer," Rory says, laughing.

"The new shirt looks nice, Roar," Mom says, smiling. "That red's a good color on you." Rory is wearing one of his five new Chaserback shirts. I only got two. Mom handed down Rory's last-year Chaserbacks to me. And Rory's old jeans, jackets, socks . . . At least she bought me new boxers.

My brother has passed along all sorts of nice things to me over the years: chicken pox, the measles . . .

"Did you brush, Rory?" General Mom asks.

"Yeah." Rory is almost out the door.

"I better smell mint." Mom sniffs Rory's mouth. "Get back up there."

"*Busted*," I say, laughing, scraping the scum off my teeth as I leave.

"Wait, guys!" Mom has the camera. "First day of school— say *cheese*."

Macy Briggs is at the corner. "We've got Bus Driver Dave this year," she says. "He gives out candy on Fridays and . . ." Macy smells like flowers. I try not to stare at the "Meow" written in silver sparkles across the front of her bright orange shirt.

The Crestwood kids are sitting in the back of the bus. They

get on first. Crestwood is right off the highway. The houses are small and close together. We used to live there, until Mom became a realtor and we moved to a bigger house in Brentwood last year. Next month, we're moving to Avalon, the nicest neighborhood of all. You have to get past a guard at the gate to get in.

Digger Jones waves to me from the back of the bus. "Hey, Mack."

Digger and I were best friends when I lived in Crestwood. We hung out every day in the woods behind his house, had dirt-bike races, built a fort. When we moved to Brentwood, Digger would come over, but Mom said I should start hanging out with Bart Schufelt and the other Brentwood kids. She said Digger was a "bad influence." She doesn't like that Digger's father goes hunting and . . .

Bart Schufelt says, "Sit here, Mack."

I do. Bart puts his headset back on. Bart's dad and mine play golf together. Bart's mom and mine play tennis. I think Bart's boring.

The bus burps and rolls again. We weave in and out of cul-de-sacs, picking up more Brentwood kids, then we cross the bridge over Maple Creek and head up the hill toward Avalon.

Bus Driver Dave stops at the gate and beeps. The security

guard wakes up and waves us through. We pass houses the size of hotels. Ours will be the smallest house on the smallest lot, but Mom says it's all about "location, location, location." Whatever that means.

Workers are swarming around our property, hammering, sawing, drilling. I get a whiff of port-o-potty. I'd hate to have to go in that thing.

Dave stops in front of the Banker mansion. It's the biggest house in Danville, with turrets and gargoyles like a castle. Out front, there's a fake lake with real swans and flamingoes, a marble fountain with five goddesses, and a tall American flag.

Pope Banker takes his time getting on. He sniffs toward the back of the bus, like he smells something bad, then takes a seat up front. Pope is new at DMS too. He used to go to a boarding school. I heard he got thrown out.

We cross back over the moat, weave through Brentwood and Crestwood again, then pick up speed as we hit the highway. I've been feeling okay so far, but when I see the building, my stomach clenches. Danville Middle School is huge.

We follow the long line of yellow buses up and around back to the unloading area, space number 47.

"Have a good one," Dave says.

"Okay, people," a teacher with a clipboard shouts. "Mohawk, red door, single file." She points to the red door.

"Oneida, blue." She points to the blue door. "Seneca, yellow." That's me. I sling my backpack over my shoulder and go.

Mohawk, Oneida, Seneca, and Cayuga are the four "houses" at DMS. I guess they figured if you divided sixteen hundred kids by four and painted each corner of the building a different color, it would feel all warm and friendly.

Seneca, yellow, yellow, yellow. I follow the yellow footprints to the yellow door. I follow the yellow arrows on the floor. The hall is jammed and noisy. I smell paint and bleach. My backpack gets shoved. I haul it back up. Yellow, yellow.

Up the yellow stairs, along the yellow walls to the long, long rows of yellow lockers. I spent the weekend memorizing "left 22, right 61, left 33." I take out notebooks for the first three periods. I'm excited to see who's in my homeroom.

After the placement letters came last month, my friends started calling to see which houses everybody had gotten into, but I thought it would be more fun to wait and see.

"What if nobody's in your house?" Rory said. Rory's in Mohawk, the red house, the one with all the best athletes. I didn't tell Rory, but I hoped I'd get into Mohawk too. "Anyone from Avalon?" Mom said. She can't wait for us to make new Avalon friends.

The bell rings. "Let's go, people," Mr. Seibel says. He's my homeroom teacher.

There are sixty kids in the room. I scan the rows, looking for familiar faces. Nobody from my old fifth-grade class. Nobody from Brentwood or Avalon, either.

The only person I recognize is Digger Jones.

CHAPTER 3
DIGGER AND SUNSHINE

My new cleats are awesome, silver fleet 2000s. Only the best for Bill McGinn's sons. Soccer was my dad's sport. Gramp made history in football, but my father picked soccer. I guess maybe he wanted to make his own mark.

Dad was ranked third nationally as a Danville junior. UCLA, Stanford, and North Carolina all offered scholarships. Dad chose the Tarheels and led them to victory four years in a row, including a double-overtime shoot-out for the US Collegiate World Cup. That game won Dad a spot on the Olympic team. Danville gave him a ticker-tape parade.

Two weeks later, the dream ended. Dad's ankle got crushed in a horseback riding accident. He never played competitive soccer again. But the bronzed cleats from that World Cup game still hang like antlers over the mantelpiece in the McGinn Museum. The Museum is where all the medals, trophies, and awards are displayed. Mostly Rory's medals, trophies, and awards. I have a lot too, but Rory's are bigger and better.

Dad loves giving his friends tours of the Museum, bragging about Rory. Dad says Rory can have his pick of colleges. Dad says Rory can make the Olympics if he wants to.

Dad coached all of Rory's teams when Rory was little, and one of mine, but then his job got too busy and he started traveling more and more.

"Listen up," Coach Barnes barks through the megaphone. "Twenty jumping jacks, then five laps to warm up. Let's go, let's go, hustle, hustle . . ."

Two hundred of us swarm onto the track. Only twenty will make the cut. There are no A, B, and C teams like in travel. There's just one Danville Middle School soccer team. Digger Jones is a few yards ahead. Black ponytail, red bandana, running like a stallion.

Coach blows the whistle. "Hit the deck, twenty-five push ups . . ."

Bart Schufelt's dad is standing next to Coach, practically kissing him. *Browner.*

"Listen up," Coach says. "Count off, one, two, three, four. Each team, take a corner of the field. Split in half, two lines facing other. Dribble across the field, then pass off. . . ."

Here we go. Right, left, right, left, side step, turnaround, fake stop. Dad says I dribble like a Globetrotter. Coach nods my way, marks his clipboard. *Sweet.*

Mom is in the stands with some of the other soccer moms. Dad calls them "Knocker Moms" because "they knock you out, they're so pretty."

"Hey, Mack-aroon!" Mom shouts to me, waving like I'm in kindergarten.

Go home, will you? How embarrassing.

I reach the other side first and pass off strong. More drills, a scrimmage, then Coach blows the whistle. "Good job, guys. See you at four o'clock sharp tomorrow."

The sports bus smells worse than a locker room. The driver's butt hangs off the seat like a ham. He doesn't smile. He's sweating. I see his name is "Harken."

"Come on, come on," Harken says. "Got to get Blondie back to the depot."

I doubt Bus Driver Harken gives out candy on Fridays.

Pope Banker looks through me, then back to his game. Bart Schufelt's got a big bag of potato chips and doesn't want company. Good. I sit with Digger.

"How'd you do, Mack?"

"I think I made it. You, too, Dig. You were wicked strong."

"Maybe." Dig gulps his water. "Hey, are you still writing that joke book?"

"Yeah, I'm trying."

"Give me one."

"Okay. How is a baseball game like a cake?"

"I don't know, how?"

"They both depend on the batter."

Digger smiles. "That's good, Mack."

Harken turns off the highway into Crestwood. He slams on the brakes.

Digger's little sister, Sunshine, is twirling like a ballerina under the CHILDREN AT PLAY sign. She has a daisy in her hair. She still has the black patch on her eye.

Harken honks the horn. Sunshine keeps dancing.

Digger's house is smaller than some of the pool cabanas up in Avalon. Cornstalks nearly touch the roof. There's the tire swing and the PRIVATE WELL sign. Sunshine's pet turtle, Go, looks up from his plastic kiddie pool. Out back, Mr. Jones is splitting logs. Behind him, the forest, our old fort, the path down . . . *Honk, honk.* Sunshine keeps dancing.

"Stupid kid," Pope Banker says. "Look at the sign: 'children at play.' She probably thinks she's supposed to play in the street. Stupid."

Bart Schufelt laughs. Harken *honk-honk-honks* again, really annoyed now. Mr. Jones comes around front with an ax in his hand. "Sunshine!" he shouts.

Sunshine freezes. She hops up onto the sidewalk.

"Stupid," Pope says again, laughing.

"Shut up!" Digger shouts, shoving Pope so hard Pope's head hits the metal bar on the seat in front of him. Pope's silver palm-port slams onto the floor and slides.

"Let's go, let's go, break it up," Harken hollers, pulling open the door.

Digger hoists his backpack and gets off.

"Digger!" Sunshine shouts, all happy, running toward him.

Digger kneels on the sidewalk. Sunshine throws her arms around his neck. She hugs him like he just got home from the Army. "Digger!" she laughs, kissing his face.

"What happened to her eye?" Pope Banker asks. His forehead is red.

I know, but I don't say anything. That's none of Banker's business. I keep staring at Digger and Sunshine. Sunshine's one good eye meets mine. She waves to me and calls my name as the bus jerks away in an angry cloud of fumes toward the bigger, better houses of Brentwood.

CHAPTER 4
GET OFF THE BUFFET LINE

"IT'S A RUN HOME."
"YOU MEAN A HOME-RUN."
"NO, I MEAN RUN HOME. YOU JUST BROKE THAT WINDOW!"

I shut off my alarm, get dressed, and sneak downstairs.

It's dark in the garage. I trip on a ball. Footballs, baseballs, basketballs, soccer, tennis, ping-pong, bowling, we've got 'em. Piled high as a mountain against the third door. If that door gets opened by mistake, there's an avalanche. All the balls come rumbling down, and the baby next door better run or get creamed.

I ease out my bike and take off. It's a short ride to the park.

The lot is empty. Good. There's a mist rising off the field. At the start of the trail, I check my watch. I've only got half an hour.

Dad and Rory are in the kitchen when I get home. They don't see me.

Dad's pointing to the face on the cereal box. "You'll be on here someday, son."

"Yeah, Dad," Rory says, "and Mack'll be on the mac 'n' cheese." They both laugh.

Butt-crack Rory.

"Don't forget you've got Blackguard tonight," Dad says to Rory.

Blackguard is Rory's premier travel soccer team. The Guards won the state title last year when Rory pulled a hat trick in the final minutes. That story got framed and hung in the "Winner's Circle," the place of highest honor in the McGinn Museum.

"Dad," Rory says. He coughs. "I'm not sure I want to do Blackguard this year."

I look quick to see my father's reaction. This isn't going to be pretty.

"I'll still do the DMS team," Rory says, "but I want to try out for hockey. . . ."

"*Hockey?*" Dad stands up. "Forget it, Rory. You're in *eighth grade* and you're still all over the place. Soccer, baseball, tennis . . . Pick one and get serious."

"I am serious, Dad. I want to try hockey."

"You're *thirteen,* Rory. Get off the buffet line and claim a table. McGinns don't play hockey. It's cold and . . ."

"*Hockey?*" Mom steams around the bend, *clickety-clack, choo-choo.* "Roar, you know the rules. No football, no hockey." She pats Rory's cheek. He pulls away. "Look at that beautiful face," Mom says. "I don't want that nose getting broken and . . ."

Two-on-one. Sweet. I feel sort of bad for Rory, though.

Rory turns and sees me. "Where were you?"

"Outside."

"How come you're sweating?"

"I'm not."

"Yeah, you are. What were you doing?"

"Nothing." I pour some juice and reach for the cereal. Rory grabs the box away.

"*What?*" I say. "What's your problem?"

Rory is pointing at my face. His eyes are squinted. His finger moves in the air like he's counting something. "Nothing," he says. "Just connecting the dots."

He's talking about my freckles. I have a lot, and they're spreading. "Shut up, Rory. Scum-breath."

"Freckle-face."

"Butt-crack."

Digger is in the last row on the bus. I head toward him.

"Sit here, Mack," Bart Schufelt calls. I sit. Bart puts his headset back on.

In Avalon, there's a limousine and a Luxury Landscapes van in front of the Banker castle. Workers are yanking out huge mounds of pink and white flowers. Crates of red and yellow flowers are standing by, waiting to take their place. Pope

Banker comes out and the limo driver opens the door for him. No bus slumming for the Pope today.

I follow the yellow road to Seneca. First period is Social Studies. Ms. Oranski-Butler, "Call me Ms. O-B," gives us our first assignment.

"Find a partner, people. Someone who doesn't live in your neighborhood."

I look at Digger and he nods.

"Go online, enter your addresses, and print out directions to your neighbor's home. Walk, bike, or have a parent drive you there. Pay careful attention; take notes. Then, using none of the usual details—no street names, mileage, route numbers, et cetera—describe in words, pictures, clay, or other fashion how to get to your neighbor's house."

"But you said don't pick a neighbor," Whitney Reed says. Whitney lives in Avalon. She and her girlfriends call themselves "the A's."

"No," Ms. O-B says, "I said don't pick someone in your neighborhood. *Neighbor* is different from *neighborhood.*"

"Yeah, right," Whitney mumbles, rolling her eyes.

"Some of you may choose to paint a picture," Ms. O-B says, "or write a song . . ."

"Oh, *please.*" Whitney makes a puking sound. I look at her. She sneers at me.

"I'm a firm believer in multiple intelligence theories," Ms. O-B says. "That's why I will always try to offer options on assignments. There are many ways of being smart. Some people express themselves better through words, some through art . . ."

I like Ms. O-B. She's a little whacked around the edges. I like that in a teacher.

After school I head out to the soccer field. There are fewer kids today. I bet some guys got spooked by the level of talent yesterday. I guess no one told them you can't just decide to start playing soccer in middle school. Some play rec soccer. "Rec" is short for Danville's "recreational teams," but rec doesn't count. If you aren't playing travel by third grade, you can forget about making the middle school team. And if you don't make DMS, no way are you making the high-school team.

So now we're down to about a hundred kids competing for twenty spots. No, actually, three spots. Rory figured out the odds. He listed all the returning eighth graders and the seventh graders who are shoo-ins because they play travel. "That leaves three spots, max, for transfers and sixth graders. Lots of luck, Mack." He didn't mean it.

My legs are sore from this morning, but I put in another good practice. Not my best ever, but I see Coach nodding my way, scribbling a few times. Digger is smokin' again today, way better than me. He's on the team for sure.

"Good effort, men," Coach says. "I'll post the list in the morning."

Everybody's huffing and sweating and looking hopeful.

"Listen, guys," Coach says, "it's not the end of the world if you don't make it. . . ."

"Yeah, right," Bart Schufelt says.

Bart sucked at soccer until his father bought him a personal trainer from Mexico. After all that pampering, even a baby could score a goal.

"You can try again next year," Coach says, "and there's always rec. . . ."

"Yeah, right," Bart says, laughing. "For losers."

Everybody laughs. I look at Digger. He shrugs his shoulders. Dig still plays rec.

Digger and I did rec together when we were neighbors. Digger's father coached. We were good. When we moved to Brentwood, though, I started travel. Digger's family couldn't afford it. It will be fun playing together again. Left wing, right wing—we'll rule.

Later, I'm up in my room doing homework when the doorbell rings.

"I'll get it," Mom shouts. I listen from the top of the stairs.

Mom says, "No, he can't." The door slams shut.

I look down from my window. Digger is speeding out of our cul-de-sac on his old trail bike. I go back to math.

The doorbell rings again. "I'll get it," Mom shouts up, annoyed.

I listen again.

"Oh, hi, Bart," Mom says, all nice. "How's your mother, honey? Come on in. Sure. Mack can come out. Mackie! Bart's here!"

CHAPTER 5
A PERFECT BRIDGE

Q. WHY DID THE QUARTERBACK COMPLAIN TO THE WAITRESS?
A. THERE WAS A BUG IN HIS SOUP-ER BOWL.

This morning, I get up fifteen minutes earlier. I get to the park and back without Rory knowing. I take a quick shower and grab a bagel for the bus.

At school, there's already a crowd huddled outside Coach Barnes's office.

"*Yes!*" Bart Schufelt shouts, pumping a victory elbow into his pudger belly.

"Hey, Mackie," he yells to me. "You made it too."

Thanks, hog-butt. Can't a guy enjoy a surprise?

Digger comes up beside me. "I came over yesterday."

"Yeah, Dig, sorry. Lots of homework."

Digger and I move in closer to the bulletin board as the guys in front of us finish looking. You can tell by their faces who made it and who's going to have a rough day.

The list is in alphabetical order. I start at the top to add some excitement, since Butt-Bart Schufelt already ruined the surprise. Cochran, J; Crupi, M; DeBattista, D; Goldman, B;

Hines, P; Kent, C . . . wait, *where's Jones?* I scan down the list . . . McGinn, M, *yes*; McGinn, R, *of course* . . . to the bottom and up again. No Jones. I look at Digger.

"Figures," Digger says and turns away.

"Dig, wait. It's a mistake." Digger was awesome. He definitely made it.

"There's no mistake, Mack." Digger kicks a locker and trudges off down the hall.

After school I bike to Crestwood, my old neighborhood, stopping a few times to make notes for the "Neighbors" project. It's warm for September, still feels like summer.

I pass by our first house, number six. It was fun living here. Gramp and Gram lived two streets over and I would visit them after school. Gramp always gave me packs of Doublemint gum. I think he liked it because it was green. Gramp was big into everything Irish. He played the bagpipes and led a march through town on St. Patrick's Day. "You're my Mack-namara," he'd say to me. "The leader of the band."

Every summer, we'd have a block party. Mr.Claminksy would fire up his Crazy Cluck barbecue truck at dawn. My mouth would be watering all morning and by noon the whole neighborhood was lined up for the "Best Cluckin' Chicken in Danville." Then, one year, somebody complained about the name, and so Mr. Claminsky changed "cluckin" to "darn." "The Best Darn Chicken in Danville." Didn't have the same ring to it, but . . .

Sunshine is sitting on the curb out front of her house, under the yellow CHILDREN AT PLAY sign. She's busy making something.

"Mackie!" she shouts, all excited to see me. "Where's Buddy?"

"He's home taking a nap. He's a lazy dog these days."

Sunshine is sad, then her face lights again. "But you're here, Mack."

"Yep." I look in the blue plastic pool. "How's Go doing?"

"He's taking a nap," Sunshine says. "He's a lazy turtle these days." She giggles and holds up a daisy necklace, like the leis Hawaiian dancers wear. "Here, Mackie."

I lean over so she can put it around my neck. There are daisies on her sneakers. "You still love daisies, huh?" I wouldn't be caught dead wearing flowers normally, but I'll wear them for Sunshine. That kid's had it rough.

"Hey, Mack," Digger comes out, surprised to see me, but glad.

A black Rover zooms past. Digger clenches his fist. "Slow down!" Go stretches his neck up and looks toward us. "Want to see the fort?" Digger asks me.

"Sure."

"Stay in the yard, Sunshine," Digger says. "Out of the street."

A big red SIR, a Suburban Island Roamer, speeds by. "Slow down!" Digger shouts. "Busy rich people speeding home to Avalon."

"*No street*, Sunshine," Digger says again. "Do you hear me? *No street*."

Digger watches Sunshine a lot. Mr. Jones works two jobs. And Dig still blames himself for the accident. He won't ever let anything happen to his little sister again.

We walk past rows of vegetables in the backyard—tomatoes, cukes, beans, lettuce—and then we are in the woods. Acres and acres of trees. A developer offered a million bucks for the land, but Mr. Jones will never sell. His wife's ashes are buried here.

Mrs. Jones was a nurse—such a nice lady, always baking cookies for Digger and me. Then her reserve unit got called up to serve in the war. Digger cried so hard the day she left, but she said she would be back soon. No. She was killed a month later in a sniper attack.

We stop by the memorial pole and the little American flag. Digger carved the pole himself, every flower, bird, and animal, all the spirits of their native ancestors.

"Come on," Digger says.

We head to the tree fort we built before I moved to Brentwood. There are four more tree houses now. "Did you build all of these, Dig?"

"Yeah." He climbs our tree and I follow. It's been a long time, but the steps we nailed in are still strong. When I reach the platform on top, I see the eagle Digger sculpted on the door. I smile and look down, remembering. *King of the forest.* Fun.

I run my hand over the initials we carved on that fire-hot August day: "DJ & MM, blood brothers." Digger and I were best friends then. It felt good to have a best friend. I made new friends in Brentwood, but never a best friend like Digger.

"Let's go," Dig says, and grabs the rope. He swings over to one of the new forts. He throws the rope back and I swing to join him. It feels great to be Tarzan again. I take a deep breath. The pine smells good. There's a cardinal on the door of this fort.

"Your carving is getting really good, Dig."

"Thanks." He swings again and I follow.

There's a yellow bird on this fort. "What's this one called?"

"Listen," Digger says. I hear the gurgling too.

"The creek's high from all the rain," he says. "Come on, I'll show you the dam."

We head down our old path to Maple Creek. The water is

running faster than I ever remember. We walk along the bank. The beaver dam is big this year, sticks crisscrossed tall as a teepee. "That's some big beaver," I say and Dig laughs.

It's quiet down here and cooler, shaded by all the trees. Digger clears skunk cabbage from the trail with a stick. I kick a pinecone across the water. Up ahead, a fallen oak tree makes a perfect bridge to the other bank.

"It came down in that bad wind storm last month," Digger says. "Now I'll have a quick way to get over to your new house in Avalon."

I try to remember what wind storm he's talking about.

"Listen," Digger says, pointing up. I hear the voices too.

On the other side of the creek, there are workers up in the Bankers' backyard. I didn't realize Avalon was so close. I know it's the Bankers from the black iron fence all around their property. The fence is electrified to keep out intruders.

A man unlocks the gate to the Bankers' pool. Two other guys hoist out a thick black hose. They haul it to the edge of the property and aim it toward the creek.

"Those a-holes." Digger is furious. "I'm calling the town."

"What's the matter?"

"They're dumping chemicals and Banker pool piss in the water. They'll kill the fish, the beaver . . ." Digger turns and bolts like a buck that smells a bullet coming.

I stand there for a minute, thinking what to do. The pool water is gushing out like a fire hydrant now. The workers sit down on the ground to watch. One of them lights a cigarette. It's five o'clock. I've got to go home.

I can't wait to tell Dad I made the team.

CHAPTER 6
"FIVERS"

Q: WHERE'S THE BEST PLACE TO BUY A SOCCER SHIRT?
A: NEW JERSEY.

"I want summer squash, pumpkin, and McIntosh." Mom is talking on the phone.

"Are you ordering groceries?" I say. "We need mac 'n' cheese and soda and . . ."

"No," Mom whispers. "Mums."

I guess it would be too simple to say yellow, orange, and red.

"Get your homework done, Mack," Mom says, hanging up the phone. "It's Gram's birthday. We'll pick up subs on the way."

Since Gramp Red died, Gram is the only grandparent I have left. Mom's mother died long before I was born, and her father lives out west somewhere. Mom doesn't speak to him. I have never met him.

Back when Mom was in high school, he gambled away all the family's money in a poker match. They had to sell their house and move into a crummy apartment. Mom was really embarrassed. Then her mother got cancer and they didn't have insurance. She died a year later. Mom has never forgiven her father for that. I don't think I'll ever get to meet him. Mom won't even talk about him.

I guess that's probably why my mom works so hard selling houses. She wants to give us more than she had. Something better.

"The candy's all ordered for Danville Day," Mom says. "It's our bicentennial year, you know." Mom is the first woman president of the Danville Chamber of Commerce. She'll be sitting on the lead float at the parade.

Danville Day is like a national holiday in our town. It's held every year on the third Saturday in November, right before Thanksgiving. There's a parade, the Turkey Trot 5K race, and a giant turkey piñata stuffed to the wings with candy. It's the biggest piñata ever. We're in the *Guinness Book of World Records.*

The winner of the Turkey Trot race gets the Golden Turkey trophy and first whack at the piñata. Gramp thought up the Turkey Trot and the giant piñata, too. Gramp was always doing good things for the kids of Danville, getting the town to build new playgrounds and athletic fields . . .

Rory won the last two Golden Turkeys.

Rory's in for a big surprise this year.

At The Yellow Submarine I order my usual, a foot-long roast beef with Russian. This was my dad's original store. Now he has Yellow Submarine franchises in seven states. Rory gets a giant meatball. Mom's a veggie wrap. The guy at the counter doesn't even ask. Between all our games and practices, we're regulars in here.

"Dad's running late," Mom says. "He'll meet us at Gram's with the cake."

When Gramp died last year, Gram moved in with us for a little while. She sold their house in Crestwood. "Too many sad memories," Gram said. Good thing she kept the cottage on Cape Cod, though. We go there with our cousins every Fourth of July.

I liked having Gram live with us. She cooked and she helped me with homework. Then one night I heard Mom say, "Bill, please, it's time. We need our own lives back." And soon after that, Gram moved into a senior center on the other side of town. At least Gram finally got a cat, Clover. Gramp hated cats. Buddy is scared of them.

We press C24 on the intercom and Gram buzzes us in. The elevator smells like medicine. Gram is standing in the doorway with her arms outstretched. "Here are my boys!"

"Hey, Gram." I hug her carefully. She's so skinny, I'm afraid I'll break her.

Rory hugs Gram too. "You're getting so big, Rory," she says.

"Happy birthday, Mary," Mom says, already checking her watch.

Gram's apartment is hotter than a Florida beach. "Is it warm enough?" she asks.

"We're good, Gram, thanks," I say.

There are two small pumpkins and some markers on the table.

"Halloween'll be here before we know it," Gram says.

"Yeah, Gram." Rory smiles at her. He opens a black marker and starts making a triangle eye. I open a green and do the same. Sometimes Gram forgets how old we are. But it doesn't matter. If Gram wants us to decorate pumpkins, we'll decorate pumpkins.

The buzzer rings. *Good, Dad's here.* I let him in.

He's carrying a shopping bag and a cake box. "How's my birthday girl?" He kisses Gram on the cheek. Clover meows and scoots under the sofa.

"There's my boy!" Gram's face lights up. Dad is Gram's Rory, her first-born son.

Dad goes into the kitchen. Mom checks her watch again. Rory and I finish the pumpkins. Gram asks about school. We hear Dad clanking around in the cupboards. "Where's the decaf, Mother?" he says. "You shouldn't be drinking high-test."

Gram winks at me. "High-test is more fun," she whispers.

"Good for you, Gram," I say. "You have whatever you want."

I go into the kitchen. Dad is sticking candles in the cake. "Mack, find me some matches, will you? I've got a meeting at seven."

"Let's go, Bill," Mom calls. "I'm showing a house at eight."

I find the matches. "Hey, Dad, guess what?"

"What?"

"I made the team."

"That's great, champ." Dad winks at me and lights the last candle. "Keep it up."

That's all? Keep it up. That's all you have to say?

The cake tastes like dirt. Gram says, "It's delicious." Mom and Dad clean up. Rory's out the door. Gram motions me to come closer. "What's the word today, Mack?"

"*Gribble.*"

"Spelling?"

"G-r-i-b-b-l-e."

"Definition?"

"Either of two small marine isopods that destroy submerged timber."

"Good, Mack. That's a fiver."

"Thanks, Gram. And it rhymes with dribble. You know—soccer."

"Soccer, shmocker," Gram says. "Soccer won't count on the SATs."

Gram used to be a teacher. She still talks about the spelling bees and "grammar grills" she did with her students. Gram doesn't think Mom and Dad put "enough emphasis on academics." She buys me and Rory vocabulary games and "word-a-day" calendars.

"Are you getting A's, Mack?"

"Yes, Gram."

"Reading every night?"

"Yes, Gram."

"Brushing your teeth?"

"Yes, Gram."

"Going to church?"

"Yes, Gram." Well, that's kind of a lie, but I don't want to scare her.

Gram squints her eyes, not sure she believes me. "Remember, Mackie: ASAP."

That's Gram for "Always Say a Prayer."

"I know, Gram. I remember."

Gram makes a big deal about looking to see if Mom and Dad are watching us. They aren't. Gram sneaks a fiver into my hand. The bill is folded into a tight, tiny square. Gram's wrinkled hand closes around my fist. "Shh," she says, touching her finger to her lips like it's a secret.

"Thanks, Gram," I say, hugging her.

"You're a good boy, Mackie. I love you."

"I love you, too, Gram."

CHAPTER 7
WELCOME TO AVALON

KINDERGARTEN TEACHER: NO, I MEAN THE REAL FOUR SEASONS. LITTLE KID NUMBER 2: I KNOW! SOCCER, TRACK, TENNIS, LACROSSE?

The Bestway vans are lined up out front. We're moving to Avalon today.

"Buddy, no!" I hear Mom shout downstairs.

Buddy bounds huffing into my room and hides behind the boxes.

General Mom storms in. "Where's that mutt?"

First, Bud's whimper gives him away; then the SBD nails him. In case you've been living on the purple bobble-head planet, an SBD is a silent but deadly fart.

"Bad dog, bad dog," Mom says, holding up a slimy chewed-up shoe. Bud hangs his head like he's sorry.

Oh, come on, Buddy, you know better. Never chew the shoes.

Bud likes to eat strange things. Tulip bulbs, a ham from a neighbor's porch, the mailman's toupee, Mrs. Trombley's black lace bra. None of which helps his digestive problems. With Buddy, we got a double hitter: drool and SBDs.

"You're staying in the Budroom in Avalon," Mom says. "Do you hear me?"

Bud whimpers yes.

Poor Buddy. Mom had the builders make a special Budroom next to the mudroom off the kitchen in the new house. Sort of like dog jail, I guess.

Bud and I get in the back of Dad's car. Rory goes with Mom in the new Suburban Island Roamer. No way was Bud going in the SIR. It has white leather seats.

I look at our house as we pull away. It's not a big tear-jerker or anything. We've only lived here a year. Macy Briggs waves as we go by. See ya later, Brentwood.

We cross over the moat into Avalon. Dad beeps at the security booth. The guard wakes up, checks our license plate, and waves us through.

The Luxury Landscapes van is back again. Yesterday, they laid down rolls of grass and made an instant lawn. Mom and Dad couldn't wait for seeds. Today the mums are going in—summer squash, pumpkin, and McIntosh. Buddy whimpers like he's scared. "What's the matter, Bud?"

Our new neighbor, Mrs. Banker—Goldie is her first name—is standing by the goddesses fountain, holding a Persian cat. I heard she has five of them. Goldie is pointing to the swans and flamingoes, talking to the cat. Goldie's long black hair is streaked with gold. They say it's real gold, painted on. The cat's diamond collar flashes in the sun. Goldie and Green Eyes stare over at us. Buddy whimpers again. Bud's a big wimp when it comes to cats. I'm not sure about swans and flamingoes.

Goldie gives a quick wet-noodle wave, kisses her cat's head, and goes inside.

Welcome to Avalon.

My new room is twice the size of my old one. I've got my own bathroom and two beds. Mom said Rory and I needed an extra bed in our rooms for when our friends sleep over. I guess Avalon kids don't do sleeping bags on the rug.

My room smells like paint. Red, white and blue paint. Mom chose a nautical theme. Gramp would have liked it. He loved boats. There are ship's wheels on the headboards. Nautical flags on the wall, spelling out something. *Mackie,* I guess. Lighthouse lamps, a navy blue trunk, Gramp's model sailboat collection . . .

I pick up the boat with the red-and-white-striped sail. The last boat Gramp and I worked on together. I rub my fingers across the smooth hull, the canvas sail. I set the boat down and turn away. *I'm so sorry, Gramp.*

I sit on my bed and look out my window, down at the deck, the lawn sloping back to Maple Creek. The water, the beaver dam, the fallen oak-tree bridge. I wonder what Digger is doing today.

"Mack! Come here!" Mom is calling, all excited.

She is spying out the front window. "It's the Banker boy. Go say hello."

"Come on, Mom, we just got here."

"Go," she says.

Mom thinks we have to suck up to the Bankers. They are the richest people in Avalon. With rich people, the richest rich rule. I still can't figure out how we can afford to live here. We are definitely the low guys on the totem pole.

I go outside to make Mom happy. She wants so much for us to fit in.

Pope Banker putts a golf ball toward the goddess statue. The ball hits a leg and bounces off the limo in the driveway. Pope sticks another ball on the tee.

"Hey," I say, and Pope looks over. He stares through me like I'm a ghost.

Pope whacks the ball again, hits a goddess in the boobs, and cracks up laughing.

I'm still standing here.

He reaches into his golf bag and pulls out a putter, a sweet one, looks like a Tiger. I turn around. What a jerk. Can't even say hello.

I'm nearly back inside when Pope shouts, "Want to see the war zone?"

I'm not sure what he's talking about. I'm about to say no when I see Mom's face in the window. She's smiling, all hopeful that I'm making friends. Behind me Pope hits the statue again. The ball ricochets and rolls into my driveway.

I pick up the ball and walk over. "Sure, I'll play."

I follow Pope past the silver knight in shining armor on his front step. A man in a tuxedo opens the door for us. Pope shoves his golf bag at the guy without saying a word. "Come on," Pope says to me.

He leads me to an elevator and presses W. "Going down."

I read the directory as we descend underground. UG 5, "Billiards." UG 4, "Spa." UG 3, "Wine Cellar." UG 2, "Arsenal." UG 1, "Security Bunker."

At "W," the elevator lands with a thud. The doors slide open.

"War Zone," Pope says, smiling.

Something about the tone of his voice makes my stomach turn.

We are in a cave. It's dark and cold. Stalagmites or stalactites—you owe me fivers either way—*drip, drip, drip*. Something flies past, squealing, just missing my eye.

"Bats." Pope laughs. "Real ones. They'll blind you if you don't watch out."

A shiver runs down my spine. Pope flips a switch and the cave lights up.

It's a gigantic laser-tag arena, ten times bigger than the one in the mall. A dark forest of winding paths and levels. *Wow.* Another bat swoops by, and I duck.

"Suit up, son, *hut, hut,*" Pope barks out a command.

"My name's Mack."

There is a long rack of black suits like something firefighters or astronauts would wear. Pope grabs one, sits on the bench, and begins to pull it up over his feet. I follow.

When I slide the mask down over my face, I feel like I'm underwater.

Pope picks a laser gun off the wall. I do the same.

Pope flicks the switch. It's totally dark.

Welcome to Avalon.

CHAPTER 8
SUCKERS,
BAITERS, DOMINATORS

Q. WHY DOES A PITCHER RAISE ONE LEG WHEN HE THROWS?
A. BECAUSE IF HE RAISED BOTH, HE'D FALL DOWN.

I stretch my hams and quads, click my stopwatch, and go.

There's the Golden Turkey running before me. Sleek as a cougar, I sprint. *Chh . . . run, run, run. Chh . . . win, win, win.* The Danville Day crowd is a blur as I bolt. *Chh . . . run, run, run.* Soon, I can't hear my breath from the cheering. *Mack-ie, Mack-ie, Mack-ie . . .* At the one-mile marker, I click my time. Shaved five seconds, more. *Sweet.*

The security guard looks confused as I bike back into Avalon. At least he's awake now. He was down for the count, chin on his chest, when I left. I hope they're not paying that guy too much.

A man in a uniform comes out of the Bankers' side gate, carrying something. Shoulders back, chin up, he marches with perfect precision to the flagpole out front. The swans and flamingoes look over. *Who the heck is he?* The birds and I watch as the man raises the flag, stands back, clicks his heels, and salutes. Then he pulls out a shiny gold bugle and starts blowing. Must be the Bankers' wake-up call.

* * *

Dad is shouting at Rory in the kitchen. "Forget it, Rory, you're going."

Dad's talking about Blackguard practice tonight. A scout from the Florida Freebirds will be there. That's the high school that recruits the best eighth grade soccer players in the country. Mom doesn't like the idea. I heard them arguing again last night. "But we live in New York, Bill, and I'm not ready to lose my son yet," she said. "He'll be going off to college soon enough."

"We can't be selfish about this, Jeannie," Dad said. "This is a chance-of-a-lifetime opportunity for Rory. I can get a condo near his campus, half my business is down South now, and we'll fly up on weekends. . . ."

Personally, I don't care where Rory goes, but what if Dad goes with him?

I stand in the hallway and listen.

"Dad, come on. I'm not quitting soccer. I just want to take a break. . . ."

"There are no breaks at your age, Rory. You're *thirteen*!"

"Dad, please, I really want to try out for hockey. . . ."

Dad stands up so fast his chair falls back and slams against the Chilean parquet. Bud barks. Dad kneels down, checking for dents. He stands up and points at Rory. "You're only as good as your last goal, Rory. Remember that."

Dad's face is red. He nods—"Morning, Mack"—brushing past me out the door.

Rory throws his cereal spoon. It lands in the sink. A glass breaks.

"Where were you?" Rory looks at me, disgusted. "Out milking cows?"

"Nowhere."

"Liar. You're all sweaty again. What were you doing?"

"Nothing."

"Loser," Rory says, getting up to leave.

Pope is at the bus stop. No limo today. I head back to sit with Digger.

"Sit here, Flack," Pope orders.

"My name is Mack." I sit down.

"Whatever." Pope squishes a bug against the window, then looks at it, dead, on his thumb. "What did you think of the War Zone?" He smiles.

"Cool." Actually, it was scary. Pope Banker likes to win his wars. I've got a bruise on my back from where he . . .

"Come over after school," Pope says. It sounds like an order.

"I can't. I've got soccer. Aren't you on a team? I saw you on the sports bus."

"No," Pope says. "I just felt like going home late. Come over Saturday, then. Blow off that stupid party. It sucks, anyway."

The Avalon Fall Frolic is all Mom can talk about. I guess it's like a block party. Mom spent days trying out recipes. We're bringing a shrimp soufflé, whatever that is. She already picked out the outfits she wants us to wear. Now she's studying the *Avalon Community Directory*, trying to memorize all of our new neighbors' names.

"That ponytail weirdo with the one-eyed sister was stalking around the back of my property last night."

Pope's talking about Digger. My body turns cold.

"Plat and I watched him on the security cameras."

Security cameras? Pope's father's name is Platinum, "Plat" for short. They say his name used to be Paulie, but he changed it to Plat when his company went platinum.

Pope laughs. He makes the shape of a gun with his hand, points the barrel forward, and squints. "That boy better watch out, or he'll find a bullet in his redskin butt."

Breakfast turns sour in my stomach. My throat tightens. I don't say anything.

"Crestwood sucks. Brentwood baits. Avalon *dominates.*" Pope nods at me, proud of his rhyme, his face all red and shiny. "Remember that, Flackie-boy."

It's Mackie, you a-hole. Mackie.

"Suckers, baiters, dominators," Pope says as we turn into DMS. "Remember that."

CHAPTER 9
REAL LIFE

In science class, Mrs. Drake says, "close those textbooks, people. You won't be needing them this year."

Sweet. Another teacher whacked around the edges. I like this school.

Mrs. Drake passes out little booklets titled, *Northern American Leaves.*

"There are two major things botanists do," she says. "We collect and we classify. You'll be spending the next few weeks outside in your own backyards, collecting and classifying Danville leaves."

"Great," Britney Scooter whispers, "our teacher's a nature freak."

Britney lives three doors down from us in Avalon. She's pretty and she knows it. She wears tops that show off her belly-button ring and skirts so short Gram would wrap a beach towel around her if she ever came to visit. Which is a possibility, because I think Rory likes her. And I mean *like* likes her.

"Your grade will depend on the quality of the specimens you collect and the number you correctly classify," Mrs. Drake says. "Thirty for a C. Forty for a B. Fifty for an A."

Fifty trees, huh? I know some trees. Mrs. Jones used to point them out to Digger and me. Maple, oak, pine, birch, willow . . .

"It may sound simple," Mrs. Drake says, "but you'll have to look closely." Her face lights up like a Christmas tree. "Just wait until you see the number of variations on the simple maple leaf, for example."

"Oh, I've got goosebumps just thinking about it," Britney Scooter mutters.

No way can I get an A if I just go collecting in Avalon. I doubt there are fifty different types of trees—maybe not even fifty trees, period. They plowed down acres of them when all the new homes went in. Good thing for Digger's woods.

At last period they let the sixth graders outside for Welcome to DMS Day. They group four hundred of us into teams for five-minute kickball games.

"When you're done, people, you can go up to the tables and get a cup of water and one ice-cream sandwich," our gym teacher, Mrs. Laird, barks through a megaphone. "One ice cream, people, *one*. The PTA is paying for this. One ice cream per person."

Digger and I sit sweating in the sun until they call our team. There are way too many kids. We don't even get a turn to kick. By the time we get to the tables, the water is gone and the ice cream is slush.

"One ice cream, Digger, one," I say. "The PTA is paying for this."

Digger laughs. "You're funny, Mack."

We sit on the grass and eat quick, vanilla dripping down our hands.

"How about this one, Dig: Why did the golfer wear two pairs of pants?"

"I don't know. Why?"

"In case he got a hole in one."

"I don't know, Mack. Maybe."

"Yeah, you're right. It's lame."

"My dad wants to do this year's rec soccer tournament on Danville Day," Digger says. "The Turkey Trot is fun in the morning, but it gets boring later. Interested?"

"Sure, I'll play." Mr. Jones has some strange ways of coaching. When he was my rec coach a few years back, he had us do these weird deep-breathing exercises. He kept telling us to "be the ball" and to picture ourselves whooshing into the net. *Score!* Mr. Jones is a little whacked around the edges for a coach, but he's good. Our team always won the tournaments.

"It sucks you didn't make the DMS team, Dig."

"Yeah. I knew I wouldn't. The whole thing's fixed."

"What do you mean?"

"Come on, Mackie, look at who made it. Every kid who did plays travel. All the parents know the coach. They were all hanging around talking to him at tryouts. My dad couldn't take off work to be there. It's like I was invisible."

"You were awesome, Dig. You should have made it."

"Yeah, there's a lot of should-haves, Mack. And then there's real life."

At soccer practice after school, I keep thinking about how Digger deserved to be there. How he's way better than Bart Schufelt. How it's not fair.

CHAPTER 10
HOLIDAY PROTOCOL

Q. WHO DID THE BATBOY WANT TO BE WHEN HE GREW UP?
A. BATMAN.

Mom is outside talking to the guy she hired to do Halloween.
Mom put out a bunch of scarecrows and pumpkins last weekend, and I thought the whole thing looked pretty good, but I
guess Goldie Banker was out walking her cats and said something insulting about it. Mom was nearly crying when she told
Dad. Poor Mom's trying so hard to fit in here.

"It has to be *big*," Mom is saying. I look out my bedroom
window to watch.

There's a girl and a black and white dog sitting in the guy's
truck. The truck is splattered with mud and missing a hubcap.
I recognize the girl, Angel Nelson. She lives in Crestwood.
She's in my English and social studies classes. The dog is barking loud. Angel sees me in the window and slouches down
like she's embarrassed.

"I want a *big* production, Johnny," my mother says. She
motions to the neighbors' Halloween displays. "I want
those giant inflatable floats, witches brewing vats of bubbling

brews, vampires coming out of coffins . . ."

Mr. Nelson says something I can't hear.

"I don't care what it costs," Mom says. "I want big. Bats hanging from trees, ghosts flying through the air, lights, music, gravestones . . . Think big, Johnny, *big*."

When we lived in Crestwood, Rory and I each carved a jack-o'-lantern for the front stoop. When we lived in Brentwood, we upgraded to an electric pumpkin and a motion-sensor skeleton that danced and sang "Super Freak."

But now we live in Avalon, and A's do Halloween big. Really, really big. Bigger than Christmas. Bigger than Disney. There's a whole section on "holiday protocol" in the Avalon *Guide to Happy Living. Protocol* is a fiver. Are you keeping track?

"Halloween displays should appear no later than October tenth. Be extravagant. Only the best for our children. And please be sure your trick-or-treaters prominently display their A buttons on costumes. As you know, Avalon has become the premier Halloween destination for vagrant gangs. Should you see an unfamiliar vehicle dropping off children, please notify Security at once. . . ."

I'm not sure if I'm trick-or-treating. I'm in middle school now. It's lame, dressing up. But then, there's the candy to consider . . . a stash to last to Thanksgiving. And forget those mini "fun-size" bars. Rory said they give out "kings" here. Okay, maybe I'll go.

"Rory, Mack!" Mom calls. "I've got an open house in Delmar. The Frolic's at three. Please make sure you're ready when I get home. I don't want to be late."

It's still early on Saturday morning. I bike to the park for another trial. Danville Day is next month. Mom showed me the Golden Turkey trophy last night:

DANVILLE DAY BICENTENNIAL TURKEY TROT WINNER

DANVILLE, FOUNDED 1808

WHERE AMERICAN DREAMS COME TRUE

When I get home, Dad is setting up the new McGinn Museum. He polishes one of Rory's trophies, puts it on a shelf, stands back, then slides it to the right. He reaches down to unwrap another from the box. So many trophies, medals, plaques.

The new Museum is twice as big as the old one. Dad had the builders add a surround-sound theater with a kitchen, bar, and bathroom. Now Dad can show his movies in style, all the legendary moments from McGinn sports history. Mostly Rory McGinn's sports history. But just wait until Danville Day.

Sunbeams bounce in off the silver and gold, filling the room with fiery bits of light. Dad sees me standing in the doorway and laughs. "Hey, we'll need sunglasses in here, huh, champ?"

"Yeah, Dad." I smile. Dad's jokes aren't funny, but he tries.

I walk in and sit down. "I think Coach might start me Wednesday." It's the first Danville Middle School soccer game. We're playing Guilderland. Our arch rival.

"Good, Mack. Bolt out there like a thoroughbred. Be aggressive. Get to the net and go for it, again and again and again. Guilderland's got a powerhouse defense and . . ."

"You're going to be there, right?"

"I'll try my best, Mack, but I've got a store opening in Georgia this week."

DMS isn't on Dad's radar screen anymore. He's focused on getting Rory recruited by the Florida Freebirds, then he'll open a bunch of Yellow Subs in Florida and . . . "But it's my first game, Dad."

"I said I'll try, Mack."

Dad never misses Rory's games. One time Rory was in a spring-break tournament and I was home sick with diarrhea. Mom was away. Dad kept calling the field to see how Rory was doing, and when he heard they made the finals, he hauled me out of bed. "You'll be all right, Mackie," he said. The bathrooms in the gym were locked. I had to go in the woods. There's no toilet paper in the woods.

Bud calls to me from the Budroom. He barks and licks my face, all happy to see me. I take him out for a walk, and then I give him a treat when we get home. "Now stay out of trouble, Bud. Do you hear me? Stay away from Mom's room, Mom's shoes, Mom's closet, Mom's office, Mom's everything. You hear me?"

Buddy sits in the corner and hangs his head, the perfect model of mutt behavior. Old Bud has me and Gramp to thank for his name. When Dad brought him home from the breeder, he named him Butler. I think Dad pictured a good dog fetching his slippers for him after a long day's work. Gramp rolled his eyes and said, "What kind of name is that for a dog? Who's your father trying to impress?"

I thought Butler was too fancy too, so I started calling him Butty. *Butty* morphed into *Buddy,* and eventually it stuck. I know it's not the most original name for a dog, but it fits. Buddy's my buddy.

I put a pan of water on the stove, open a box of mac 'n' cheese, and then check my assignment notebook. Math sheet, Spanish quiz, "Neighbors" project.

After lunch I bike to Digger's, double-checking the landmarks. The tennis courts, the clubhouse, the sleeping guard in the security booth, the bridge over Maple Creek moat, down the hill into Brentwood, past the big willow, Woo, on the corner of Walden, then straight on to Crestwood.

Smoke is coming from Digger's chimney. It was chilly last night. They burn wood for heat. I knock on the door. Digger looks surprised. "Come on in, Mack."

I haven't been inside this house in a long time. It smells like smoke and something sweet. Sunshine's daisy plants on the window ledge. Digger's carved animals on the mantel. Shiny black deer eyes peering down at me.

"I'm baking a cake," Digger says. "It's Sunshine's birthday."

"How old is she now?"

"Five."

I remember when Sunshine was born. Digger carried her across the street in a wicker basket to show me. She looked like a kitten. Her hair was silky black and she had the biggest brown eyes I'd ever seen. I know Dig will never forgive himself for what happened to her eye on that camping trip.

"The 'Neighbors' thing is due Monday," I say.

"Yeah, I finished." The oven buzzes. I follow Digger into the kitchen. He sticks a toothpick into the cake, pulls it out, and looks at it. "That's how you test if it's done," he says. "I'm a regular chef these days, Mack. Pretty soon, I'll have my own TV show."

I laugh. "Yeah, right."

"I will. You wait and see. Are you still living off mac 'n'

cheese?" Digger hands me a plate of cookies. They're a weird green color, but I try one.

"These are good." I take two more. "What's the green stuff?"

"Zucchini."

"*Zucchini*. That's nasty, Dig. Who ever heard of zucchini cookies?"

"Anybody who's got fifty ripe zucchinis sitting on the counter."

Every bit of counter space is covered with vegetables. It's like the produce section at Savemore. Fat red tomatoes, bunches of carrots, cucumbers, peppers, corn.

"I'll be cooking this weekend," Digger says. "Soup, chili . . ."

Digger's family always has a big garden. Mr. Jones fishes trout in the spring, bass and sunnies in the summer, and hunts turkey and deer in the fall. He freezes stuff to last all year. I tried the deer meat—venison—once. It wasn't too bad. *Venison* is a fiver. They've got blackberries, raspberries, and an apple tree. About the only food they buy is milk and cheese. They even had a goat when we lived here, but somebody called the town to complain. I still think it was my mother.

"Dad's doing a practice for the Danville Day team next weekend."

"I'll be there," I say. "And come on over later if you want. I'll be home around five. It's the Avalon block party. I'm going for the food and blowing off the rest."

As I'm leaving, I see the locked case, the guns and bows. The old wooden sign on the wall. BEAVERBROOK, HOME OF THE IROQUOIS, 1708.

Danville used to be Iroquois land until the pilgrims pushed the Indians out. Danville, founded 1808. Where American Dreams Come True.

CHAPTER 11
WATER-BALLOON WAR

Q. WHY ARE TENNIS PLAYERS SO COOL?
A. BECAUSE OF ALL THE FANS.

"Let's go!" Mom shouts. She's dressed in a fancy blouse and skirt. I thought this was a picnic. Rory's arguing about clothes. Who cares, why bother? I put on the shirt Mom laid out on my bed. This block party is like travel team tryouts for her.

"First impressions are everything," Mom is saying to Rory.

Mom is dying to impress Goldie Banker. Goldie Banker decides which Avalon mothers are "in" or "out." My mom is a Blue Ribbon real estate agent, the first woman president of the Danville Chamber of Commerce, but that doesn't mean anything here in Avalon. In Avalon, Goldie Banker is queen. Queen Goldie says who's in or out.

There's a big white tent over the tennis courts; a band is setting up. We are the first ones here. Mom puts down the shrimp soufflé. We fill out name tags.

"Be sure your sons get A buttons for Halloween," a lady with very blond hair says. She doesn't introduce herself. "You can pick them up at the Clubhouse."

The food is way too fancy. No hotdogs, no burgers, no nothing like the Best Cluckin' Chicken in Danville. And it's all little kids. I don't see anybody my age.

Later, when it's crowded, I sneak away. Rory left a long time ago. Mom is talking with some ladies, inching closer to Goldie Banker. Come on, Goldie, give my mom a break. She worked hard to get on the A team.

Digger rings my doorbell at five. He's holding a bag of water balloons. "Dad got these for Sunshine, but I was afraid Go would eat one and choke."

Sweet. I haven't done water balloons in years. If it doesn't involve a ball, a team, and a trophy, McGinns don't play.

Outside, we can't find a faucet anywhere.

"Big place like this," Digger says. "How do you water your flowers?"

"Sprinkler system. Come on. We'll fill them up inside."

"Are you sure?" Digger says. "Won't your mother be mad?"

"We'll be careful. She won't know."

Digger leaves his sneakers by the door. He starts filling balloons in the kitchen. I take the guest bathroom faucet. Bud *woofs* from the Budroom.

"Sorry, Buddy, you can't come out. Can't have you eating balloons."

Rory comes down. "Cool," he says. The doorbell rings.

Two of Rory's new Avalon friends, Andy Slater and Matt Gleason. They walk right in without taking their shoes off.

"Water balloons," Rory says, laughing.

Andy and Matt each take a handful of balloons and go upstairs to look for faucets. Rory gets one of the cardboard moving boxes and we start piling in the fat, wet balloons.

"Oh, yeah," I say. "This is going to be awesome." Digger doesn't look so sure.

Andy and Matt are laughing loud upstairs. "Holy sh--," one of them says.

The doorbell rings again. I answer it.

It's Angel, the girl in the truck from this morning, standing there looking scared.

"You're in my English class, right?" she says. Angel has pretty eyes, curly brown hair, and freckles. "Do you have the *gum?*"

"What gum?"

"The *GUM*, the *Grammar Usage Manual*. We've got a vocab quiz Monday."

Angel's cute. I can't just tell her to leave. "Come on in if you want."

Woof. Oh, no. Someone let Buddy out. He bolts by, huffing around the bend, slip-sliding in a pool of drool, paws tap dancing on the Chilean parquet. Mom's going to kill me. Bud's barking happy like he just broke out of jail. He leaps up the thick pink carpeted stairs, two at a time, two at a time. *Oh, please, Buddy, not the shoes.*

Andy and Matt come in with armfuls of balloons. Rory gets another box.

"We've got enough now," Digger says. "Must be a hundred here."

"Wait," Andy says. "We've got a bag of balloons at home. I'll be right back."

Andy brings two more packages. Rory gets out more boxes. We keep filling and filling and filling and filling and filling. Hundreds and hundreds of balloons. We're all laughing crazy now. This is going to be the best balloon fight ever.

"Come on," Digger says. "We're making a mess. Let's take it outside."

"We can't," Rory says, standing by the window. "Look."

Two Chemgreen trucks are parked out front, red lights swirling on top like police cars. Four guys in green suits with masks get out. They strap metal tanks onto their backs.

"Plat Banker called Dad this morning," Rory tells me. "He saw a little hole on our front lawn and freaked. 'Grubs! Grubs!' he screamed into the phone. He told Dad to call the Chemgreen Emergency Hotline. 'Got to smoke those suckers out.'"

The Chemgreen guys divide to conquer. They face the four corners and begin the attack, spraying every inch of Banker and McGinn terrain, smoking those suckers out of their holes. Another guy follows behind them, sticking orange flags along the borders. PESTICIDE APPLICATION. DANGER. NO CHILDREN OR PETS FOR 24 HRS.

"Oh, great, now what are we going to do?" I look at the clock. Mom and Dad will be home soon. The bell rings again. I answer it.

Pope Banker is mad. "I told you to come over, Flackie."

Pope looks at Digger like Digger is dirt. "What are you doing here?"

"I'm Mackie's friend," Dig says.

"That's right," I say.

Pope looks at me funny. Then he sneers at Angel. She backs away, spooked. Pope turns like he's about to leave, and then he spies the boxes. The hundreds and hundreds of water balloons. He makes this evil smile.

"War!" he shouts, scooping up ammo. "You call the teams, Lackey."

"It's Mackie."

Rory, Matt, and Andy come in to the kitchen.

"Good," Pope says. "The As against the suckers."

That's Digger, Angel, and me. Before I can speak, Pope lobs one at my face. It stings, and cold water slides down my shirt.

"Are you sure you want to do this, Mack?" Digger says.

I hear the A team's feet pounding up the stairs. "No choice now, Dig."

"Come on, then, let's go." Digger picks up a box of balloons. Angel and I follow. We stand crouched in the hallway. My chest is pounding.

And then it's totally quiet. So quiet, you could hear one of Bud's SBDs.

Quiet, quiet, hearts pounding. *POW!*

Smack, boom, pow! Smack, boom, pow, splash, splash . . . Sweet. Balloons blasting from every direction. Water, water everywhere. The As have the advantage of higher ground. But I know the lay of the land. "There's another staircase on the other side. Come on, Angel, let's go."

Digger's trapped downstairs, but he uses his bow-and-arrow arm to pummel them. Angel and I sneak up. I surprise-attack Rory. Andy creams Angel. Pope misses Dig by a mile. Buddy's barking but I can't see him. There's water everywhere, like it's raining. We're laughing. This is awesome. Then I hear the security signal, *beep, beep, beep.* The front door opening. Women's voices. Everybody freezes.

"Yes, thank you, Goldie." It's my mother talking. *Oh, no.*

"We were very pleased. It's Chilean inlaid parquet. Thanks, that's kind of you to say. Oh, yes, I'd love to see your kitchen. I've heard such wonderful . . ."

And then there's a cat-curdling, brain-busting scream.

Goldie Banker is peeling a pink water balloon off of her forehead, black mascara dripping on her cheeks.

Pope is looking down, laughing hysterically, like it's the funniest day of his life.

"Oh, Goldie," my mother says, horrified. "I'm so sorry."

Bud whips in, slip-sliding in the water, freaking crazy he's so happy to be free, and drops something on Goldie Banker's bare feet as he crosses. Goldie picks it up, screams, and flips it away. It skitters across the floor. A jockstrap.

Goldie pats the top of her head. "Oh, my God!" she screams. "Something's dripping on me!"

"Holy sh--," one of Rory's friends shouts. "I forgot to shut off the faucet."

My mother looks like she's in a horror movie. Her mouth is open, but no sounds are coming out. And just then, Digger comes around the corner.

My mother turns on him and screams, *"You! Get out of my house."*

CHAPTER 12

GROUNDED

HOW DID YOU BREAK YOUR ARM?
I TACKLED A SODA MACHINE.
WHY DID YOU DO THAT?
TO GET THE QUARTER BACK.

"You're grounded for a week," General Mom says. "No TV, no games, no music. And you are absolutely forbidden from hanging around with that . . . that . . . *delinquent*."

It's nearly midnight, and we just finished picking up all the little pieces of balloons, strewn like wet confetti throughout the house. Mom couldn't get ahold of our cleaning lady, Vega, because it's the weekend, and we couldn't find a mop anywhere, so we've all been on our hands and knees on the floors, soaking up water with beach towels, Dad practically crying about the Chilean parquet.

Rory's in trouble too, but not like me. Mom blames the whole thing on Digger.

"But, Mom, it wasn't Digger's fault."

"Where did the balloons come from, Mackie?"

"Well, Digger brought the first bag and we tried finding a faucet outside but . . ."

"Case closed," Mom says.

"Pope Banker started the war."

Mom flinches at the Banker name. I can tell that the whole awful scene is flashing across her mind in every, single gruesome detail. "Oh, I'm so embarrassed," she sobs, sinking into a chair, her face in her hands. "I am ruined in Avalon, and we just moved in! Do you realize what you've done? Goldie Banker will never forgive me."

"Mom, why do you hate Digger so much?"

Mom springs up like a cheetah. "Well, let's see, Mackie. Why don't we start with the thousands of dollars' worth of water damage to the ceiling, or the mud stains on the rugs, or the—"

"Mom, wait. Digger was the one trying to get us to go outside. But we couldn't because of the Chemgreen. . . ."

"And let me see what else." General Mom is on a roll. "I told you I didn't want you hanging out with that boy. All the guns in his house . . ."

"Mr. Jones hunts for food, that's all."

"It's barbaric, Mack. And dangerous. You know how I feel about guns."

I think about the Arsenal on Underground level 2 next door, but I know better than to throw lighter fluid on a campfire.

"And have you forgotten, Matthew . . ."

Oh, boy, she hasn't called me that in years.

". . . about what happened to that poor girl . . ."

"Mom, stop." I'm angry now. "That wasn't Digger's fault."

"Stay away from him, Mackie. I mean it."

Just then, Bud makes an appearance. He's been hiding somewhere all night. He brings the jockstrap over to Mom and drops it by her feet like a peace offering.

"And you!" Mom shouts. "You're not a dog, you're a . . . demolition derby." She yanks Bud by the collar and pulls him into the Budroom. Poor Buddy whimpers like *I'm sorry, but what did I do?"*

"I warned you, Buddy. I've had it. . . ."

"Leave him alone, Mom. He's just a dog. He was just having fun."

"*Fun!*" Mom shouts, her face fuming red. "Well, the fun is over. A dog like that doesn't belong in a house like—"

"So what are you going to do, Mom, huh?" My heart is pounding. "Get rid of Bud like you got rid of Gram?" And as soon as the words come out, I freeze. It's like I'm transported to another dimension where I can't see or hear. I'm afraid to look at her.

Mom hurls another wet towel toward the laundry room. "Go to bed," she says.

"Mom, I'm sorry."

"And set your alarm for eight. Tell Rory, too. We're going to church tomorrow."

There's only one worse fate than being grounded, and that, is it.

CHAPTER 13
MAGGIE CARROLL'S
SERMON

BOXER #1: DO YOU WANT A KNUCKLE SANDWICH?
BOXER #2: NO, THANKS, I'M A VEGETARIAN.

Whoever named this church Our Lady of Perpetual Sorrows wasn't kidding. The sorrows are perpetual, all right. They go on and on and on. *Perpetual* is a definite fiver, and you better pay up. If you cheat a guy on Sunday, it's a double sin.

Why is Our Lady of Perpetual Sorrows so bad? Well, first there's the bad breath and farts and sticky-finger babies pulling at your hair. Then there's the longer-than-the-Bible prayers that all sound the same. *Blah, blah, blah, blah, blah,* AMEN. And then there's the music that would make Buddy howl if he were here. And you can just forget about taking a nap. Catholics aren't stupid. They keep changing positions to keep you awake. Stand, kneel, sit. Sit, stand, kneel. Sit, stand, sit, stand, kneel, stand, kneel . . .

There are three guys up on the altar today. Father Teddy; he's okay. The deacon who never smiles. And a fat priest I've never seen before. I can tell he's a priest because he's wearing a cape, a really fancy one.

The deacon is giving the longest sermon ever. "Remember the prophet Ezekiel," he says. *Blah, blah, blah, blah, blah, blah, blah.* He looks perpetually sorrowful. That must be how he got the job.

It's hot. I'm hungry. The baby behind me just dropped another fish cracker down my back and now she's fishing for it. The deacon *blahs* on and on and on. I check Dad's watch. It's been over an hour.

"AMEN."

Good, that sounded like the final AMEN. The Amen, Amen, we're-outta-here Amen. Then, just when I think they're springing us free, Father Teddy announces "and we have an honored guest with us this morning. Father Ralph Frangipani, Director of Diocesan Vocations."

That's *vo*-cations, not *va*-cations. There is a huge difference. *Vocations* is a fiver. And don't forget, it's Sunday.

Father Ralph waddles to the podium. It's about five steps from his chair, but he's out of breath when he gets there. You can hear him huffing into the microphone. He's got fat neck rolls like a sumo wrestler. "Dear brothers and sisters in Christ." His voice booms so loudly he scares the fisher-baby behind me. The baby starts to cry. "Our beloved church is in a crisis, the depths of which we have never experienced in the history of the papacy. There is a critical, *critical* shortage of priests in our country . . ."

He looks at me and then at Rory.

". . . and the number of young brothers entering the seminary has plummeted . . ."

"Well, then, let the sisters in," Mom mumbles.

Dad looks at her. "*Shhhhh,* Jeannie." He hates when Mom has opinions.

"Well, I'm right," Mom says. She crosses her arms and scowls.

Sumo Priest bellows on and on and on. I look up at the blue statue of Mary, the Mother of Jesus. She's crying, frozen in marble, perpetually sorrowful.

Sumo Priest says, "Soon, our beloved American churches will be completely run by foreign-born priests, many of whom don't even speak English." He shakes his head woefully and wipes his sweaty forehead.

"Parents, I implore you," Sumo says. He looks right at Mom. "Please pray for vocations in your family. It is imperative that you do all that you can to encourage your sons toward the priesthood." He looks at Rory and me again. "There was a time in this country when every family was honored to send one of its sons to the seminary . . ."

"This guy's whacked," Rory whispers to me.

Sumo Priest booms on and on. My stomach is growling. My

whole morning is shot. I'm ready to blow like a volcano. *Ground me for three weeks if you want, four, five, but please, please, please, let me go.* The deacon looks like he might keel over from the sorrows. Father Teddy is our only hope. He is the only one who can make Sumo Priest sit down. But Father Teddy is too nice. He sits there, calmly listening, like he's got nothing better to do. I am trapped in perpetual sorrow.

Then something amazing happens. Something exciting. And, believe me, nothing exciting ever happens at Our Lady of Perpetual Sorrows. It's a miracle or something.

Over in the far right corner by the choir, there's a commotion. I nudge Rory to look. A short woman stands up, says "Excuse me, excuse me," and makes her way out to the aisle. Once she hits the rug, she's off, strutting fast and determined toward the altar, arms pumping at her sides like the grayheads power walking at the mall.

"What the heck is she doing?" Rory says.

By the time the short lady reaches the front, the whole church is watching her. She bows low at the foot of the altar, makes a big sign of the cross, and then power pumps up the three steps to the microphone.

Sumo Priest is so shocked, he stops talking. *Good.* Short Lady says something, and Sumo bends down to listen. Then Sumo backs away and the lady takes the microphone. Her face is round and kind and she's smiling like she won the lottery. She looks to one side of the room and slowly moves her head, making eye contact and nodding to people in every section of the church like she wants to make sure we're all paying attention.

"That's Maggie Carroll," Mom whispers to me. "She has Down's syndrome."

Now Maggie Carroll looks scared, like she just realized what the heck she's doing. There are rules about these things. You can't just walk up on the altar in the middle of mass. Maggie looks over at Father Teddy. Father Teddy smiles at her.

Then Maggie Carroll clears her throat, takes a deep breath, and shouts: "Feed the hungry."

That was it. The whole speech.

The church is so quiet, you could hear a fish cracker drop.

Maggie Carroll hands the microphone back to Sumo Priest. She gives a great big wave to someone in the audience. She struts down the steps, bows low, then power walks back to her seat, arms whipping like little windmills.

After church I see Maggie Carroll. I think about congratulating her on the really brave thing she did. That was the shortest, sweetest sermon I ever heard.

An old man and woman, must be Maggie's parents, each take one of her arms and start shuffling her toward the door. They look embarrassed or angry or something. Not Maggie, though. Maggie is smiling like it's her birthday, like she won the lottery on her birthday. She sees me looking at her. "What's your name?" she says loudly.

"Mack. Mack McGinn."

"Hi, Mack Mack McGinn," she says.

"I liked your speech," I say.

"I like you, too, Mack Mack McGinn."

CHAPTER 14

**KINDERGARTEN TEACHER: PLEASE. CAN'T ONE OF YOU NAME THE FOUR SEASONS?
LITTLE KID NUMBER THREE: NASCAR, WATERSLIDES, DIRT BIKES, POOL?**

On Monday it's raining, but I bike to the park anyway. The ground is slippery, but good for training. By Danville Day, the trail will be covered with wet leaves.

I stretch out, check my watch, and bolt. I take a deep breath; the rain feels good. My legs are strong, stride is good, arms propelling me, eyes on the prize. *Phhh . . . run, run, run. Phhh . . . fast, fast, fast. Phh . . . win, win, win.*

I picture Maggie Carroll, arms pumping her forward, so brave and focused and determined. I hope you didn't get in too much trouble, Maggie.

It's raining. We have a substitute bus driver. When she stops for us, she's talking with the dispatcher, looking over a list like she's confused.

"Sit here," Pope Banker says. I do.

"The water thing at your house was bush," Pope says. He

starts laughing. "Except for seeing Goldie's face. *Smack—Bull's-eye!* That was worth the whole . . ."

The bus driver heads down through Brentwood, but instead of going straight to the highway, she turns back into Crestwood and stops at Digger's house.

Digger is hunched under a little yellow umbrella that Sunshine is holding for them. Digger has to practically kneel on the wet ground to fit under it. Sunshine looks proud to be in charge.

"Thanks for coming back for me," Digger says to the bus driver. He flings water off his long black hair and adjusts his red bandana.

"No problem," the driver says. "It was my fault."

"Hey, Mack." Digger nods at me. He starts to sit in the empty seat in front of me and Pope, but Pope slams his book bag down onto it.

"It's saved," Pope says.

Digger looks at Pope. Digger looks at me. I look at Sunshine, still watching us as she twirls her umbrella. Digger moves on back to find another seat.

"Somebody better tell that boy where his kind are supposed to sit," Pope says.

I shiver. I don't say anything. I should defend my friend.

* * *

At school there are posters for the DMS Roadrunner on Friday. It's a one-mile cross-country race. Anybody in the school can enter. The winner gets a blue ribbon and one thousand points for his or her house. Second place gets the red and five hundred points. Third place gets yellow and one hundred.

The four houses compete for points all year—math challenges, science quests, jeopardy games, sports contests, canned food drives—and the house with the most points at the end of the year wins a trip to Escapades Waterslide Park. The one thousand points from the Roadrunner is usually a good indicator of which house will win the trip.

I think about entering, but if I do, then Rory will see how fast I've gotten. He'll know that I can beat him in the Turkey Trot on Danville Day. Too bad, though. It would be sweet to win one thousand points for Seneca house. I'm starting to like it here.

When I walk into Social Studies, Digger looks at me and turns away. I feel bad. I should have stuck up for him on the bus. Ms. O-B tells us to join our partners in front of our "Neighbors" projects. Mine is a three-dimensional diorama. It's a definite A. I was proud when I finished it last night. But now I don't feel so proud.

"Dig . . ."

"Save it, Mackie."

"Dig, I'm sorry. . . ."

"Forget it, Mack." Digger is mad. "If you can't talk to me in front of your new neighbors, don't talk to me at all."

Ms. O-B is looking at our work. "Now, isn't this interesting," she says to me and Digger. "How two people can see things in such different ways? Look, Mack, you say it takes you ten minutes to get to Digger's house. But Digger says it only takes him two minutes to get to yours."

I look at Digger's project. He drew it on a brown-paper grocery bag, burned around the edges to look old, like a bark map. There's Digger's house. I can tell by the daisies and the PRIVATE WELL sign, the tire swing and cornstalks. I follow the arrows around to the vegetable garden and into the woods behind . . . past the totem pole . . . past the tree forts, eagle house, cardinal house, bluejay . . . down the path to Maple Creek, the teepee-shaped beaver dam . . . across the oak-tree bridge and up the bank on the other side. The Bankers' black iron fence is on the right. An X on the left marks "Mackie's house."

We both get A's.

After school is our last practice before the first DMS game.

Coach Barnes divides us in half for a scrimmage. Rory and I are on the same team.

"Rory, right striker, Mackie, left. Let's see the McGinn brothers in action."

The play is fast. I bolt down the field. I'm wide open. "Pass, Rory, pass!"

Rory acts like he doesn't hear me. He barrels toward the goal. *Score.*

"Why did you hog the ball?" I ask Rory later.

"To get the job done."

"But I was wide open."

"I play to win," Rory says.

"But I had a great shot. You could have passed."

"What's wrong with you, Mackie?" Rory looks disgusted. "Grow up. This isn't kindergarten. You get the ball, you go for the goal. Nobody remembers assists, Mackie. They only remember the goals."

CHAPTER 15
"Mack-ie, Mack-ie, Mack-ie . . ."

KID: HEY, COACH, CAN I PLAY WHEN MY CAST COMES OFF?
COACH: I DOUBT IT. YOU COULDN'T PLAY BEFORE.

Rory and Dad are arguing in the kitchen. "No, Dad, I can't blow off the game."

Our first DMS soccer game is today at four. Coach Barnes is starting me and Rory, left and right forward. I'm the only sixth grader starting.

"*Rory.*" Dad is mad. "Freebird tryouts are at six o'clock. It's going to take us forty minutes to get there. I don't want you all tired out. You've got to be in best form. You only get one shot at this."

"But, Dad, I can't let down my team."

"*Rory.*" Dad's voice is rising. "This isn't a joke. Who cares about a middle school soccer game? You have a chance at the premier high school team in the . . ."

"All right," Rory says, "all right."

"Be ready at five," Dad says, just as I come into the room.

"But, Dad," I say. "Can't you still come watch some of my game? You could pick Rory up at school."

"Sure, Mack," Dad says, sighing like he's tired. "I'll do my best."

"I'll be there," says Mom.

"Yeah, okay," I say. I want Dad to come.

"I'll pick you up at the soccer field at five then, Rory," Dad says. "But I don't want you playing. Do you hear me? Stay on the bench. Conserve your energy."

Angel Nelson sits down in front of me in English. She turns around and asks what I'm writing. I show her my joke book.

"That's cool," she says, smiling. She turns back around.

I tap her on the shoulder. "Want gum?"

She looks confused. "The *Grammar Usage Manual*?"

"No, the real stuff." I hand her a pack of watermelon Bubbagood.

She laughs and takes a piece. "Thanks."

Angel is wearing a plain yellow shirt and blue jeans. No jewelry or makeup. There are rainbows and flowers drawn on her sneakers. I never saw a girl draw pictures on her sneakers before. Maybe Angel's trying to start a trend. I doubt anybody's going to copy her, though. Crestwood girls don't start fashion trends. Avalon girls do.

"I'm sorry about what happened at your house with the

water balloons," Angel says. "What a mess. No wonder your mother was so mad."

"It's not your fault," I say.

"But why did she blame Digger? It was Pope Banker's idea."

"It's a long story. Mom just doesn't like Digger."

"I think Digger's nice," Angel says. "When we moved into Crestwood, Digger's family made us feel welcome. They brought over a plate of cookies . . ."

"Were they green?"

"*Green?*" Angel scrunches her nose. "No, yuck. Chocolate chip."

"Yeah, Digger's a good guy. My mom doesn't understand."

"Where did he get the name Digger, anyway?" Angel says.

"When we were little, he was always digging in the woods behind his house. He said he was looking for a deerskin pouch full of gold coins that his great-great-great-great grandmother buried right before the massacre of . . ."

"Good morning, everyone!" Mrs. Schmidt, our English teacher, comes bubbling into the room, especially excited today. Mrs. Schmidt loves books. I mean, this lady really loves books. I think she loves them more than weekends or people or food.

"We have a new project," Mrs. Schmidt says, smiling, clasping her hands together. "I'm sure that during your elementary school years you wrote an autobiography, and I'm sure you've done family trees. You probably know a lot about your mother and father and siblings, but, for this assignment, I want you to pick another relative and tell us his or her story."

I don't have to think too long about this one. I'll write about Gramp.

After school I head to the locker room to suit up. Rory is getting changed too. So much for the Freebirds. I don't say anything. Dad is going to be wicked mad. *Good.*

It's warm for October; there's a bright blue sky. The Knocker Moms are in the bleachers with their cups of coffee and plastic horns. *Oh, please, Mom, don't embarrass me.* I search the faces for Dad.

We take our places on the field. I jog in place. I'm feeling good. I look over at Rory. This is the first time I've ever played on a soccer team, or on any team, with my brother. I'm excited. We're going to win. I search for Dad, but I still don't see him. I try to get Rory to look at me, but he's staring down a forward on the Guilderland team.

The ref calls and the goalies wave in ready. The whistle blows and we're off. Guilderland has control of the ball, but not for long.

Bart Schufelt blocks and sends it back our way. I've got a huge Guildy player on me, definitely an eighth grader, but I kick the ball loose, trap it, and loop around past him.

"Mackie, *pass!*" Rory yells. I do.

Rory scores. The first goal of the season.

The crowd goes crazy. "Ror-y, Ror-y." The Knocker Moms blow their horns.

And then I see my dad. He's standing with Coach Barnes. Coach pats Dad on the back. Dad is staring at Rory, nodding his head, smiling proud, hand cupping his chin like he's trying to be modest. *Yep, that's my son. That's my star.*

I could have had that goal. Why'd I listen to Rory?

Our defense wins the ball back. There are midfielders ready to do the job, but Andy Slater kicks the ball all the way up the field to Rory. I head in to assist.

The Guildy defenders are all over Rory. I'm open. I've got a sweet shot.

"Rory!" I shout. Rory is trapped. He slips and loses the ball for a second.

"Rory!" I yell.

The Guildy guard on Rory is big, and he's not backing down. I'm wide open. I see Dad, tense, hands on his hips. "Rory," I shout, "pass, *pass.*"

And just then, Rory breaks free. It's like he's the only guy on the field. It's like he's talking soccer to that soccer ball and that soccer ball is listening.

The crowd is screaming. Two Guildy defenders are on Rory, and he's nearly out of bounds. Then, suddenly, Rory stops. He turns and kicks in a sweet leftie, almost as sweet as a header. The ref blows the quarter whistle. The crowd goes wild. "Ror-y, Ror-y."

That's okay, shake it off. I've still got three quarters to show Dad my stuff.

Coach huddles us in for a talk. "Let's go—one, two, three, D!" We head back out to the field. I'm pumped to score the next goal. And that's when I see Dad and Rory, leaving. Dad's got his arm around Rory's shoulders. Freebird tryouts.

I'm almost crying; such a lamer. Dad could have stayed longer if he wanted to.

Bart Schufelt takes Rory's position. Bart nods at me like "Let's do it."

Guilderland strikes back hard. By the fourth quarter, we're tied, 2-2. The pressure is on. Two-minute warning. The ball is in Guildy's strike zone.

I bolt like a tiger, steal the ball, and dribble it home to Danville. "Who's that?" someone says. "Rory McGinn's little brother," somebody answers, as I barrel past. I run like I'm alone on the field. Like I'm on that trail in the morning, just me, running, heart pounding, wind in my ears . . . and when the coast is clear, I kick it in. . . .

Score.

Sweet.

The ref blows the final whistle. My team comes running. They hoist me up in the air. Bart Schufelt's almost crying he's so happy. Coach is smiling like it's summer vacation. People are cheering, "Mack-ie . . . Mack-ie . . ."

On the sports bus home, I sit by myself, looking out the window.

Everybody saw I'm not just Rory's little brother.

Everybody saw me win big.

Everybody but my dad.

CHAPTER 16
PEACE OFFERING

KNOCK-KNOCK.
WHO'S THERE?
URIAH.
URIAH WHO?
KEEP URIAH THE BALL!

"Congratulations, Mack," Mom says at home. "Awesome game."

"Thanks." I drop my gym bag, head into the Budroom, and slunker down on the floor. My dog knows just what I need right now. A welcome-home slobber. No talking.

"What's wrong?" Mom asks.

"Nothing."

"Well, something's wrong, Mack. Aren't you happy? You won the game. On *your* goal. What a way to start the season. Coach Barnes was thrilled."

"Yeah, whatever." I rub Bud's coat. He licks my face. Thanks, Bud. I can tell Mom is watching me.

"I don't ever remember Rory playing that well as a sixth grader," she says. "All of the parents were impressed. Some lady said, 'Who's that kid?' and I said, 'That's my son. . . .'"

Mom stares at me until I look at her. "What?" I say. "*What?*"

"I know you're disappointed Dad had to leave."

"He didn't *have* to leave. Freebirds didn't start until six o'clock."

"I know, Mack, but I'm sure Dad wanted Rory to have time to shower and change and eat some dinner. And you know how slow Rory is getting ready . . ."

I stand up. "Yeah, I know. I know all about Rory." I kick my gym bag across the floor. Bud barks. Thanks, Buddy, you're always on my side.

"Hey, listen," Mom says, all cheery. "Why don't we go out for dinner?"

"No, thanks."

"Come on, just the two of us, Mack. It will be fun." Mom sounds like a little girl.

"No. I've got too much homework."

I go upstairs and take a long, hot shower, change into sweats, and lie down. Later, when I wake up, it's dark. Mom is knocking on the door.

"Yeah, what?"

"I brought you dinner."

"Thanks, Mom. I'll get it in a minute."

Mom doesn't answer right away. "Okay, Mack. I'll leave the tray right here. But don't wait too long. It will get cold."

I'm starving. As soon as I hear her leave, I open the door.

There's the wooden tray Mom used to bring my birthday breakfast to me on when I was little. She'd put a candle on top of a big stack of pancakes and she and Dad would wake me up singing. "Happy Birthday to . . ." I'd blow out the candle and they'd sit on the edge of my bed drinking their coffee while I ate. I don't remember when they stopped doing that.

I reach down for the tray. There's a roast beef sandwich with Russian, a bag of barbecued chips, two cans of root beer, and a big bowl of mac 'n' cheese, still steaming hot. Now that's what I call a peace offering. Except Mom's not the one who hurt me.

"Thanks, Mom," I shout down the stairs.

"You're welcome, Mack," she shouts back up.

Later, when I bring the tray down, I see Mom peeking out the living room window. "What are you looking at?" I say.

"Goldie's having her Pampered Pooch tonight."

"Her what?"

"Her Pampered Pooch party. I saw the invitation at Ella Slater's house. Pampered Pooch carries the top boutique lines of holiday clothes and accessories, toys, gourmet edibles, bubble baths . . ."

"For dogs?" I say.

"Cats and dogs."

I think to myself, *that Banker lady is whacked,* but I see how sad Mom looks and I don't say anything. Mom is still on Goldie Banker's "out" list.

"Don't worry, Mom," I say. "She'll forget about the water-balloon thing."

"I hope so, Mackie."

"Besides, Mom, we don't need any Pampered Pooch stuff, anyway. Bud's got everything he needs. Right, Bud?"

Bud woofs right on cue and slunkers back off to dog dreamland.

I turn on my computer and stare at the blank screen. I type "Mrs. Schmidt, English 6 A, Relative Story," and then I sit there. I think about Gramp for a long, long time. Finally, I start to type: "My grandfather, Jack 'Red' McGinn, was a hero. You may know him as the famous football player who built all the playgrounds for kids in our town. There is a statue of him in Danville Park. But I knew him as my grandfather, someone who was always there for me. . . ." I stop. I click SAVE.

I lie down on my bed. *You were always there for me, Gramp, but on that last night, when you needed me, I wasn't there for you. I just couldn't say good-bye. . . .*

CHAPTER 17
THE GOLDEN TURKEY

Dad and Rory are still at the Freebird tryouts.

"I've got an eight-thirty showing, Mackie," Mom calls up to me. Fall is a busy time in the real estate business. Mom says people are hoping to make their dreams come true by the holidays. "I'll be home in an hour," she says.

I've got the house to myself.

Rory's room is a mess. Mountains of dirty clothes and wet towels, pizza boxes, candy wrappers, soda cans on the floor. When Vega cleans Rory's room, she shakes her head like mad and mutters in Slovak. Every once and a while I'll hear some English—"pig" or "slob" or "big pig slob."

I head straight for the prize: Gramp's football. The one he carried tucked under his arm when he ran sixty-three yards for the Fightin' Irish in the most famous game of his career. I turn the old ball slowly in my hands. I take a deep breath of leather. I rub the ball against my cheek. I hug it tight as a teddy bear. *Gramp.*

When Gramp died, I got his model sailboat collection. Rory got the football.

"I asked Gramp if I could have it," Rory said. I still don't know if that's true. All I know is that I didn't go into the room at the hospital that last night when they called us all to come. Gram was sobbing in the hallway, Mom and the aunts trying to comfort her, Dad and the uncles trying to look brave. All the cousins sitting on the floor, looking like refugees.

Everybody went into Gramp's room, one by one, taking turns saying good-bye.

Everybody but me. I went somewhere else. If I didn't say good-bye, then Gramp wouldn't go.

I walk downstairs to the Museum. Dad has the lights dimmed to keep all the gold and silver from tarnishing. I turn up the lights. There are the Golden Turkeys Rory won the last two Danville Days. Gramp invented the Golden Turkey, and the giant piñata, too. Gramp used to say, "Give a kid a game and some candy and he's golden."

Only one kid wins the Golden Turkey, but everybody gets candy when the turkey piñata cracks. Gramp had the piñata especially designed by a toy company. I don't know how many pounds of candy they stuff into that gargantuan bird. That's right, *gargantuan* is a fiver. That turkey piñata's bigger than a float in the Macy's parade.

Give a kid a game and some candy and he's golden, right, Mack?

Right, Gramp.

Rory thinks the Golden Turkey trophy is lame. He makes fun of it every year. Rory doesn't care. Rory's got Gramp's football.

I hear Dad and Rory come in, and I head to the kitchen. Mom walks in too. "Perfect timing," she says.

"You should have seen this guy." Dad is slapping Rory on the back, bragging to Mom. "He blew the other kids right off the field. The Freebirds coach was so impressed, he came right up to me afterward. 'Mr. McGinn,' he said, 'I can't promise anything until we finish the recruitment tour, but I have to tell you that your son is one of the finest forwards that I have ever . . .'"

"Oh, Rory, that's great," Mom says. She doesn't sound too excited. She doesn't want Rory to go to Florida next year. Florida is a long way from New York.

"Mack had a good night too," Mom says, winking at me. "Go ahead, tell them."

"Yeah, I scored the . . ."

"They showed us a film," Rory interrupts, all-pumped-up

happy. "The school is right near the ocean, awesome beach, everybody was surfing . . ."

"Rory," Mom says, but he just keeps on bragging.

". . . and there's a food court right on the campus, anything you want—burgers, tacos, Chinese, frosties—and twenty-four-hour pizza delivery right to your room . . ."

"*Rory,*" Mom says, smiling. "Your brother has some good news too."

Rory looks at me. "Hey, how'd we do?"

"We won."

"Sweet," Rory says. He's actually smiling at me.

"How'd *you* do, Mack?" Dad says.

He means, did I score. I stare at him but I don't say anything. I feel like spitting at him.

"Mack scored the winning goal!" Mom shouts. "You should have seen him, Bill. It was tied right up until the final minute, and then Mackie blasted from the pack. Coach Barnes said, 'That's quite an athlete you've got there. . . .'"

"That's great, champ," Dad says, swiping the top of my head like I'm four. I can tell he's still thinking about what the Freebirds' coach said about Rory.

"We'll know by Thanksgiving if he got accepted," Dad says.

My second of glory is over. "I'm going to bed."

It's all about Rory again.

CHAPTER 18
THE ROADRUNNER

After my run on Friday morning, I'm biking back up our street when I see the guy come out of the Bankers' side gate and march out front past the goddess fountain and the fake lake. He pulls the ropes to raise the flag, stands back, clicks his heels, and salutes. Then he gets his bugle out.

At the sound of the music, one of the swans lifts its long neck, spreads its wings, and rises up to fly. It gets just so far up off the ground, then jolts to a stop. It struggles briefly in midair. I see the glint of the silver wire that *tethers* the bird's skinny leg to the ground. Yep, tether is a fiver. Good, you're getting the swing of this.

Vega told me the wires are how the Bankers keep the lake birds from flying away. Vega cleans for the Bankers. The Bankers have a live-in maid. Vega just does the "Girls' Suite." The Girls are Goldie's five Persian long-hair cats. Each cat has a princess bed, grooming station, and private litter box. Goldie's Girls wear tiaras and diamond collars. Their names are Fir, Her, Myrrh, Purr, and Sir. Don't ask me how Sir got her name. I don't have a clue.

Vega has her own names for the cats. She shows me the scratches and nip marks. Trust me, Vega knows a lot of good Slovak swears.

"Are you doing the Roadrunner?" Rory asks me at breakfast.

There's a new bucket of bubblegum vitamin balls. We both take green.

"Yeah, probably." I'm not, but I don't want Rory to get suspicious.

"Mohawk House always wins," Rory says.

"Who took first last year?" I ask.

"Danny Hodgkinson," Rory says. "But he graduated. I've got it this year."

I put peanut butter on a bagel. I don't say anything.

Dad sips his coffee, still smiling about Rory and the Freebirds.

"Are you coming to the Roadrunner?" Rory asks Dad.

"Wouldn't miss it," he says. "You're going to win this year, right?"

What about me, Dad? I feel like he punched me. *How do you know I wouldn't win?* Sixth, seventh, and eighth graders all run together. It's anybody's race. *You're just so sure about Rory, aren't you?* My heart is pounding. My face is getting red. I was going to hold back until Danville Day, but, you know what, I'm going for it today. The big win. Then another on Danville Day. A one-two punch. *Just wait until you see me, Dad. Just wait until you see me beat Rory.*

In Social Studies, Ms. O-B announces that the "Neighbors" projects were so good that she's decided to do a "Neighbors, Part 2" called "Trading Places."

Kids groan. "Part one was enough," Diva Landerly complains.

Diva lives in Avalon. I remember her partner was Angel Nelson. What's wrong with Angel? She's nice.

"It's one thing to know where a person lives," Ms. O-B says, "but as the famous Native American saying goes, you can't judge any man until you have walked two moons in his moccasins."

"I'm not wearing Angel Nelson's moccasins," Diva whispers to her friend, Whitney Reed, loud enough for others to hear. Diva and Whitney crack up laughing.

I look back at Angel. Her face is red and her eyelashes are beating fast, like she's trying to blink back tears. She picks up a pen and starts doodling. I look down at her white sneakers, all covered with happy little things.

"We will, of course, need the cooperation of your parents,"

Ms. O-B says. "I am sending letters home this week. With their permission, I want you to trade places with your neighbor for one moon—twenty-four hours. Try to live for a day exactly as he or she would. Sleep in her room, eat with his family, do her homework, his chores, her sports, extracurriculars . . ."

No way is Mom going to let me trade places with Digger. I look over at Digger. He's looking at me. I can tell he's thinking the same thing.

After school I change into shorts and my running shoes. It's a perfect day for a race. Cool but sunny, no wind. Our gym teacher, Mrs. Laird, showed us the Roadrunner route the first week of school. I know it by heart now. Around the school parking lot, up the hill, through the woods, down around the football and soccer fields, and up the steep bank to the finish line. One mile, cross-country. Easy.

There are hundreds of us lining up to run. Everybody else is hanging out to watch. I see most of my teachers, lots of parents.

I take the position I want, on the far left. It will shave off a few seconds when we round up toward the woods. I stretch my hams and quads, roll out my shoulders and neck, jog in place, take some good, deep breaths. My heart's pounding, excited. I was going to hold off until Danville Day to make my big move, but . . .

"Gook luck, Mack-aroon!" Mom shouts.

Please stop calling me that. I don't look to see where she and Dad are standing. I don't look to see where Rory is or Digger or anyone else. When I run, I don't want any distractions. When I run, it's just me. Face forward, feet on fire, eyes on the prize.

"Positions," the principal barks through a microphone.

The pack shuffles and leans forward.

"Ready . . ."

For a second, it's stone quiet. . . .

Boom.

I tear off like a panther, eyes on the prize, feet on fire, *fast, fast, fast.* The blue ribbon dangling before me, one thousand points for Seneca. *Chhh . . . fast, fast, fast,* strong strides, powerful pace. I maneuver to the front. *Pound, pound, pound, pound,* the sound of sneakers on the path. As we round up toward the woods, there are about thirty runners out ahead of me. Digger is one of them. So is Rory, but I'm not worried. The hill is steep and high, and then there's the deep drop. The change in terrain will knock lots of guys out. It's the ups and downs that make or break a runner.

Chhh . . . fast, fast, fast. Chhh . . . win, win, win. Nimble feet in the woods, watching for holes and tree roots, eyes on the prize, *fast.*

Out of the woods I speed down the hill, passing runners with every exhale. When I turn toward the soccer fields, it's flat and wide open, and I let go, full steam.

Feet on fire, feet on fire, I pass Digger, then Rory, then one, two, three, four more. I'm out front now, eyes on the prize, blue ribbon for Seneca. *Faster, faster, faster, faster* . . . I can't hear anyone behind me. . . .

"Mackie." It sounds like Rory.

"Mackie!" It *is* Rory, but I'm not turning around.

When we were little and racing somewhere, like home for dinner or to the ice-cream truck, and Rory wanted to get there first, he'd point to the ground and say, "Hey, Mackie, is that your candy? Hey, Mackie, is that your quarter?" trying to get me to stop and look so he could run past me and win.

I'm not a stupid little brother anymore.

Faster, faster, feet on fire, hot, hot, hot, hot, hot . . . I finish the loop and bolt up the hill, the crowd cheering on either side. I wish I could see Dad's face.

"Mackie!" Rory shouts.

No way am I looking.

"Mackie, watch out . . . to your left!"

"What?" I turn and Rory whizzes past me, across the finish line. *First.*

CHAPTER 19
BIG TOUGH GUY

"Shut up, Rory," I say again.

We're eating dinner and Rory keeps trying to talk about the race. I can't look at him or I'll explode. I took Buddy out for a long walk to burn off steam when I got home, but I'm still seething mad. *Seething* is a fiver, ya got that?

"The red ribbon's good, Mack," Rory says. "You still got five hundred points."

"Shut up, Rory. I mean it."

My voice is so loud, I scare Buddy. He stands and shakes his head side to side, flinging drool everywhere. He barks from the Budroom gate, staring intently at me. Bud knows something is wrong.

Rory's all happy, shoveling spaghetti into his mouth, tomato sauce dripping down his chin, gloating in his blue-ribbon glory.

I think about how that race was all mine and then I turned, *I turned,* something you never, ever do in a race, and in a flash Rory flew by me across the finish line. And then all the cheering, the wild war cries from Mohawk house, teachers and kids slapping him on the back, Dad and Mom hugging him so proud . . . the principal handing Rory the blue ribbon, cameras flashing . . . "*Cheese!*"

"You were burning rubber today, Mack." Rory throws me a pity bone. He looks over at Mom like *See, I'm being nice to him.* "When did you get that fast?"

"Shut up, Rory. I'm warning you."

"Come on, guys, let's eat," Dad says.

"Here, Mackie." Mom passes me the garlic bread. I don't take it.

"Hey, Mack, I'm sorry," Rory says, making a gurgling sound too close to the sound of a laugh. "But I was just kidding when I kept calling you. I didn't think you'd actually turn around."

Now Rory's really laughing. "Hey, Mack, remember when we were little and we'd be racing somewhere and I'd call your name and . . ."

I spring out of my chair, brain bursting with anger, and punch him in the face.

Rory looks stunned as his chair topples backward, like he can't believe this is happening, like he can't believe I really hit him. The chair crashes loud on the parquet floor. Rory lies there. He touches his nose, looks at the blood . . .

Mom rushes over to him. "Rory, are you all right?"

Rory's still in shock. My heart's pounding like a drill. "Rory, I'm sorry. I didn't . . ."

And then Rory's face changes. "I'm going to kill you, Mack."

Rory rises up, blood dripping, lunging toward me like a bull.

"Stop it!" Dad shouts. He grabs Rory's arm.

"Leave me alone," Rory says, yanking his arm away.

I clench my fists and stick out my chest. "Come on, Rory, come on."

"Matthew," Mom says. "I'm ashamed of you. Stop it."

Bud's barking like crazy, running in circles, pushing against the Budroom gate.

"It's over," Dad says. "The two of you. Go to your rooms *now*."

My heart is pounding. My head is pounding. I've never punched anyone before.

"Big tough guy, huh," Rory says, elbowing me hard as he pushes past me up the stairs, nose in the air to block the bleeding. "You're dead, Mack."

For hours I lie on my bed, heart pounding, head pounding. I hate Rory.

That race was mine. Rory didn't need the Roadrunner. He's got the Freebirds. He's got Gramp's football. He's got Dad. . . .

And then the big, tough guy cries like a baby.

You are such a loser, Mackie.

CHAPTER 20
THE CIRCLE

Q. WHAT DO YOU GET WHEN YOU CROSS A HOCKEY PLAYER WITH A GROUNDHOG? A. SIX MORE WEEKS OF HOCKEY.

When I show up for practice for the Danville Day rec soccer team with Digger and Mr. Jones, all I can think of is that old *Bad News Bears* movie. Let's just say, we're not talking travel team material here.

There's nothing bad-news about Mr. Jones, though. He's a nice guy. I've never once heard him yell at Digger. And he's in good shape for a dad, strong from delivering furniture all day and hauling slabs of beef around a meat-packing plant at night.

Digger looks just like his father. They have the same long black hair and brown eyes. Mr. Jones talks in a slow and calm voice. "Let's sit in a circle, everybody."

The ground is damp. It's windy. Summer's definitely over.

"This team is a circle," Mr. Jones says. "A circle is round." He makes eye contact with each one of us as he looks around. "A circle has no beginning or end, no first or last, no winner or loser. We're all equal here."

I look around at my teammates. No one is making puke faces or saying "Yeah, right" or "Give me a break." There are kids I used to hang out with when I lived in Crestwood: Taylor, Louis, Noah, Lathisha Green, Raul. Some new Crestwood kids: Janell, Mecca, and Nigel. Nigel's a good player. And then there's Angel Nelson. Angel smiles at me. She's wearing red cleats, no pictures on them.

Mr. Jones makes each of us say our name and then has everybody else repeat it. "The first thing I want you to do is to learn all of your teammates' names," Mr. Jones says. "Communication is key in soccer. I want to hear you talking to each other out on that field."

We do jumping jacks and run around the track. Coach Jones sets out the orange cones on the field and works us through the usual warm-ups and drills. He splits us up for a scrimmage. All regular practice stuff. But then Mr. Jones does something I've never seen another coach do.

He squats down and pulls out a clump of grass. He holds it up to show us. "If you're going to play soccer, you've got to be ready to run. And runners need to know if the wind is on their side."

I look over at Digger. He must get his running talent from his father.

Digger is staring at his dad like he's proud of him, like it isn't lame at all to be watching your father holding grass up in the air in front of all your teammates.

Mr. Jones wasn't at the Roadrunner yesterday. He didn't see Digger beat out hundreds of other kids. He didn't see his son win the yellow ribbon and one hundred points for Seneca. Mr. Jones isn't one of those parents who can take the afternoon off to watch his kid's game. Not when you've got two jobs you can't. Actually, three: furniture lifting, meat packing, and taking care of his family.

"Look." Mr. Jones holds the grass up high, then lets it fall. We watch the breeze carry the green wisps to the left. "Now you'll know when your side has the advantage."

After practice Digger and I go out to the woods behind his house. We've got our *North American Trees* manuals and bags to collect the leaves.

Digger has been working on the forts since I was here last time. There's a new ladder on that one, a new roof over there. I move toward the fort with the yellow goldfinch on the door. I have been conditioned to move toward yellow. Yellow, yellow, yellow.

Conditioned is a fiver. How much do you owe me, anyway?

"What are you going to do with all these houses, Dig?"

Digger picks up a big brown leaf and studies it. "Red oak,"

he says. He pokes holes for eyes, nose, and mouth and looks through the mask at me. We laugh. Digger picks up another red oak leaf and gives it to me.

"Thanks." One down, forty-nine to go for an A.

"I'm making them for Sunshine," Digger says. "When she goes to school next year, she and her friends can play here."

I look at the forts, the Tarzan ropes. It still looks good to me, but I guess Digger's right. Tree houses are for little kids. We're in middle school now.

"It might be fun, though," Digger says, "to have one last, big camp out back here, maybe before it gets too cold. . . ."

"Yeah, that sounds great," I say. "Who are you going to invite?"

Digger thinks for a minute. "How about our rec soccer team."

"The girls, too, or just the guys?"

"What?" Digger laughs.

"Are you going to invite the girls to sleep over too, or just the guys?"

"Well, there's four houses," Digger says. "Two for us, two for the girls. We'll take Eagle house. Unless, of course, you want to sneak over and scare Angel Nelson in the middle of the night."

I look at Digger. He laughs. "Race you to the creek," he says.

CHAPTER 21
ROSA PARKS

Q. WHAT DO YOU SAY AT THE START OF A FLEA RACE?
A. ONE . . . TWO . . . FLEA . . . GO!

Chh . . . fast, fast, fast. Chh . . . win, win, win. I run the trial with my best time yet. *Sweet.* It's October twenty-fourth. Three weeks until Danville Day. *Gobble, gobble,* here I come. That Golden Turkey is calling my name. I'm holding Gramp's trophy high in the air . . . the piñata cracks open . . . the candy rains down. Dad will be smiling, all proud. "Say, cheese, Mack! *Cheese.* Where did you learn to run like that, son?"

"Winning runs in the family, Dad. Get it? Winning *runs* in the family."

When I get home, Mom is standing in the front doorway, looking all upset. "We didn't get spooked last night," she says.

"What?"

"It's an Avalon tradition. The week before Halloween, a neighbor comes at night, tapes a paper ghost on your door, and leaves a bag of candy. There's a letter that says, 'You've been spooked and now you have to spook three more neighbors tomorrow night.'"

"So?" I still don't get it. "What's the problem?"

"Last night was the *first night*. I heard Leona Faddegon talking about it at the Club. She was ordering special orange-and-black chocolate truffles to put in her kids' bags. That seemed a little overboard to me, but . . ."

"Don't worry about it, Mom. We'll probably get spooked tomorrow."

"That's too late, Mack. Anybody's who's anybody gets spooked the *first* night. Why don't you ever invite Pope Banker over? Or Bruce Faddegon or that Elliot boy? You have to make an effort, Mackie. You can't just expect kids to start including you."

At the start of social studies the next day, Ms. O-B is standing in the classroom doorway. "You sit in the back today," she says to me in a mean voice. "You sit in the front," she says nicely to Nigel.

"How did that feel?" Ms. O-B asks when everyone is seated. "Did you like being told where to sit? Imagine if there were laws that told you where you could or couldn't sit based on the color of your skin?"

I look at the kids up front. I wonder what Nigel and Janell are thinking right now.

Ms. O-B clears her voice. "Today we will study one of the brightest lights in American history. Rosa Parks, the mother of the civil rights movement."

Rosa Parks was the brave lady who wouldn't give up her seat on the bus.

Mrs. O-B adjusts her glasses and reads: "Rosa Parks, a black seamstress whose refusal to relinquish"—I told you *relinquish* would come in handy—"her seat to a white man on a city bus in Montgomery, Alabama, grew into a mythic event that helped touch off the civil rights movement of the 1950s and 1960s. . . ."

Ms. O-B talks about segregation. *Segregation* is a fiver, but I'll give it to you for free in honor of Rosa Parks. We actually had these whacked-out laws here in America to keep black and white people separate from each other. There were different schools for black kids and white kids, separate water fountains, toilets, sections in restaurants . . .

"Mrs. Parks's courageous nonviolent act inspired a twenty-six-year-old preacher named Martin Luther King," Ms. O-B goes on. "The Reverend Jesse Jackson said that Rosa Parks 'sat down in order that we might stand up. . . .'"

The fire alarm blares loudly and I jump. The principal's voice comes over the intercom. "Faculty, code orange, please assist your students in exiting the building."

"Okay, everyone," Ms. O-B says, "please stand and calmly, *quietly*, follow me."

I don't smell smoke. I hear hundreds of footsteps through-out the school, all of us heading outside. We walk to the back soccer fields and wait. There are three fire trucks and a bunch of police cars, lights flashing, out front.

Bart Schufelt's class is next to mine. "Hey, Mack, did you hear about the soccer tournament at Danville Day this year?"

"Yeah. I'm playing."

"With who?" Bart asks, all nervous, like he's scared he got left out or something.

I tell Bart about Digger's father's team.

"You're kidding." Bart laughs. "What are you doing on a Crestwood team?"

"Playing soccer."

Eventually, they let us back into the school. Nobody explains what happened.

All afterschool events are cancelled because tonight is Open House. I'm nearly to my bus when I remember I need my math book. I go back inside, and as I'm coming out, I see Pope Banker leaving the principal's office. We both just make it to the bus. Digger motions to come sit with him and I walk back to join him. Angel Nelson smiles at me.

Digger and I make plans for the camp-out.

"How about Halloween night?" Dig says. "There's no school the next day."

"Sure, sounds good." I'll ask Dad. Mom would never say yes.

The bus stops near Digger's house and the driver honks the horn. Sunshine is dancing in the street again, under the diamond-shaped sign. I wish she wouldn't do that. All those cars speeding past.

Sunshine's wearing a long pink dress and crown, waving a sparkly wand, probably testing out her Halloween costume. She runs toward Digger. He kneels down for a hug. Sunshine says something. Digger closes his eyes. Sunshine laughs. She swirls the wand above Digger and then bops him on the head.

"What were you doing back there?" Pope says to me when we get off the bus.

"Where?"

"As sit in the front. Cs in the back. Remember that, Flack."

The door to the Banker mansion opens. Pope's father is standing there with his fists clenched. "Get in here," he shouts to Pope. "Now."

I head up my driveway, but turn back to look just as Mr. Banker yanks Pope's arm and slaps him across the face. I wonder what that's all about.

Later, the phone rings. Mom knocks on my door. "It's for you, Mack." She has her hand over the receiver. She looks all excited.

"Come over," Pope Banker says.

Mom is standing there looking hopeful.

"Okay," I say. I really don't want to.

The butler answers the bell. "Follow me," he says.

We pass by a huge pink room with crystal chandeliers and classical music playing. There are five pink satin beds with names inscribed in the crowns above them: *Fur, Her, Myrrh, Purr,* and *Sir.* Myrrh looks up at me and snarls as I walk by.

Upstairs, the butler knocks on a door. "Master Banker, your guest is here."

Pope is standing by the window looking through a telescope—a serious telescope, like the kind they have in planetariums. You can probably see Uranus with that thing.

But Pope isn't looking up at the sky. He's looking down.

"Check this out, Flack," he says.

"It's Mack," I say. "Mack."

I look into the telescope. There's Digger. He's sweeping out Cardinal House.

"What's that redskin doing?" Pope says.

"I don't know," I say, my heart beating faster.

"What are all those forts for?" Pope says.

"I don't know."

"Well, somebody better find out."

CHAPTER 22
HALLOWEEN IN DISNEYLAND

Q. WHAT IS A GHOST'S FAVORITE POSITION ON A SOCCER TEAM?
A. GHOUL-IE

Avalon looks like Disneyland, every house decked huge for Halloween.

Mr. Nelson got everything Mom ordered, and more. Flying witches, ghosts swinging from trees, Frankenstein, and a graveyard. It's the biggest, best show in Avalon. People are even calling to congratulate us.

The letter from Ms. O-B came today about the "Neighbors" project, part two. I told Mom how Digger and I are supposed to trade places for a moon, but Mom is so happy, she isn't even complaining. She was mad when she came home from Open House and saw my diorama and Digger's map—"Why did you pick him?" she said—but the "Neighbors" project isn't on Mom's radar screen anymore. There was something else in the mail today. Something more exciting. An invitation from Goldie Banker. She's having a birthday party for The Girls— their royal highnesses, Fur, Her, Myrrh, Purr, and Sir. Our whole family is invited.

Mom is buzzing around like it's the happiest day of her life, doing Internet searches, calling gift consultants to find the perfect presents for the cats next door. A lot depends on those presents. They are Mom's ticket to the A list.

Mom is grilling Vega for insider information on Fur, Her, Myrrh, Purr, and Sir. Vega is mopping the floor, shaking her head, mumbling Slovakian swears. I bet Vega has some good ideas for gifts, all right. She hates those cats.

Dad gets back from Sam's Club with the trick-or-treat candy bars. Mom looks in the bags. "They're too small," she says in a panic. "Take them back, quick. It's almost dark. Get the king-size, Bill, the bigger the better, and get a lot of them. Hurry!"

Diva Landerly's mother, the lady with the very blond hair who was so rude to us at the Fall Frolic, stops by to compliment Mom on our Halloween spread and to drop off A buttons for me and Rory to wear trick-or-treating tonight.

"I edit the *FAM*," Mrs. Landerly says, "the *Family Avalon Magazine*. I'm sending by a photographer to capture your house today, if that's all right, Mrs. McGinn. This is just the sort of grand-scale holiday imagining we pride ourselves on here in Avalon. And you are just the sort of family we want to showcase. We can't *wait* to see how you do Christmas!"

Pope Banker calls to ask if I want to hang out with him

tonight. "I've got a case of Silly String," he says, laughing. "Six cartons of eggs, red spray paint . . ."

I tell him I have other plans. I don't tell him I'm going to Digger's.

Pope is mad. I don't think he has any other friends.

When Dad gets back with the king-size bars, I say, "The soccer team's all crashing together after trick-or-treating." I don't say it's the Danville Day rec team.

"If it's okay with your mother, sure."

I tell Mom that some neighbors are having a sleepover.

"A sleepover?" she says. "Wonderful!"

I know she thinks it's in Avalon. She's happy I'm finally fitting in.

Rory heads out with Andy and Matt. They're meeting their girlfriends down behind the clubhouse. Rory's got a gorilla mask and a pillowcase for candy in his hand, but I know he's not going trick-or-treating. He'll be face-sucking behind the tennis courts with Britney Scooter as soon as it gets dark.

"Have fun, Rory," Mom says. "Don't stay out too late."

"Yeah, have fun, Rory," I say, laughing, making a kissing sound. I put on my costume and shove a sleeping bag, blanket, and flashlight into a bag. "See ya later, Mom,"

Pope Banker yells over to me as I'm biking off. "Where are you going, Flack?"

"My grandmother's. She gets scared on Halloween."

* * *

A police car passes slowly down our street. By the security booth, there are two more patrol cars and four officers with walkie-talkies. Probably on the lookout for trick-or-treater intruders. They'll smoke those suckers out of Avalon tonight.

Who cares? So what if kids come here for candy? It's Halloween. It's their night.

The guard in the booth is wide awake for once. "Where's your A badge?" he asks.

"Home."

"You can't trick-or-treat without it."

"I'm not trick-or-treating. I'm going to my grandmother's house."

Brentwood is decorated for Halloween too. Not as big as Avalon, but still pretty big. Trick-or-treaters pass me. Macy Briggs is dressed like a cheerleader. "Hi, Mackie," she calls, and her girlfriends giggle.

When I get to Crestwood, Princess Sunshine hugs me. "Kneel down, Mackie," she says, all excited, holding her wand up in the air.

"Close your eyes." She's giggling. "And make a wish. But don't say what it is."

"Okay, Sunshine." I wait a few seconds to play along. "Okay . . . I've got it."

"Good." She whacks me hard on the head. "Your wish is granted."

Digger is the Hunchback of Notre Dame. I'm a soccer player. I know. It's lame.

We meet up with Nigel, Noah, and Raul. Nigel's a football player. Nigel's playing it safe too. Noah and Raul are rappers. We hit every house in Crestwood.

Most people hand out "minis," except for the dentist who gives us toothbrushes and the pretty lady who gives out paper bags filled with caramel popcorn.

"That's your girlfriend's mom," Digger says. "Mrs. Nelson."

"Shut up," I say. "She's not my girlfriend."

Digger rings the bell at a small brown house on the end of Elm Street. I don't remember ever coming here before.

Maggie Carroll answers the door. She's dressed in an old faded wedding gown that's way too big for her. "Mommy," she shouts. "It's Mack Mack McGinn."

My friends snicker behind me. Digger tells them to shut up.

Maggie puts a candy bar in Digger's pillowcase. She puts five in mine.

"Happy Halloween, Maggie."

She laughs and pulls me toward her. She plants a big, slobbery kiss on my face. "Happy Halloween, Mack Mack McGinn. Happy Halloween."

The soccer team meets up at Digger's house at ten o'clock. Mr. Jones is leaving for work. "Sunshine's asleep," he says, shutting off the front porch lights, "so keep the volume down." He looks at Digger and smiles. "There's snacks and soda in the cooler."

"Thanks, Dad," Digger says, "and don't worry. I'll keep checking on Sunshine."

We flip on our flashlights and head out to the woods.

"I'll start a fire," Digger says. "Angel, you and Janell and Latisha take Cardinal House. It's the biggest. Come back down when you're settled."

"I call Bluejay," Nigel says. He starts up the ladder, and Raul and Taylor follow.

"We'll take Eagle," Digger says to me. He throws me his backpack and I climb up and lay out our sleeping bags.

I stand on the platform and take a deep breath. Most of the trees have shed their leaves. The woods feel closer to the sky. There's the Big Dipper. And there's the Little. I haven't seen them in a long time.

Digger has a good fire roaring in the old stone pit. The

wood hisses and crackles. I open a can of soda and claim my spot.

It's quiet except for the cars zooming past every so often on the street out front. An owl hoots. A squirrel, or something, rustles in the leaves.

Angel sits down next to me. "I've got a joke for you," she says.

"Okay."

"Why is a baseball diamond better than a football field?"

"I don't know, why?"

"Because diamonds are forever."

"That's a good one. Girls will like that. Okay if I use it?"

"Sure." Angel smiles at me.

When everybody is settled around the campfire, Digger starts telling stories. First, a scary one about a psycho doctor who carves out peoples' eyes on Halloween night. Then an Iroquois legend about a girl who flies on a turtle's back. Nobody tells a story like Dig. It's in his blood or bones or something.

It's getting chilly. The girls are yawning. Angel smiles at me.

"It's late," Digger says, kicking dirt on the dying embers.

Dig and I head up to our fort and dig in to the Halloween candy. "It was a good night, huh, Mack?"

"Yeah, Dig. Just like old times."

I wake up, cold, in the dark. There's a light flashing around outside, then a spraying sound. "Dig," I say, but he's snoring loud. I hear somebody laugh. A mean, evil laugh. I know that laugh. My heart is pounding. I start to move, but my body feels heavy as a house. "Dig," I say louder. He keeps snoring. What should I do? I fumble for a flashlight. All I can find is the candy. The noises stop. Whatever Pope did, it's over. We can't do anything tonight, anyway. We'll deal with it in the morning. I toss and turn all night. My eyes are closed but my ears are pricked up like a forest animal, listening. . . .

CHAPTER 23
GROWING UP FAST

KNOCK-KNOCK.
WHO'S THERE?
JOSÉ.
JOSÉ WHO?
JOSÉ, CAN YOU SEE, BY THE DAWN'S EARLY LIGHT . . .

In the morning, there's Silly String everywhere. Slimy pink and yellow strips all over the ground, dripping from the trees. Mrs. Jones's memorial pole is covered with red paint. The flag is in the dirt.

Digger is kneeling by the pole. His shoulders are shaking. I leave him alone. A guy doesn't need somebody talking to him when he's down that low.

Angel, Nigel, Noah, all of us pick up the strips of Silly String. Nobody says anything about the pole.

"Who would do such a cruel thing?" Angel whispers to me, her eyes filled with tears.

My stomach clenches in a fist. I know who.

We clean up as best we can in silence, then Digger says he has to get breakfast for Sunshine. We pack up our bags. I bike home. What should I do? Who I should tell? Pope Banker can't get away with this.

* * *

When I get home, General Mom's in the kitchen, barking orders into the phone. "I want twenty miniature fir trees with twinkle lights—no, make that fifty trees for the front driveway, wreaths with red velvet bows in each window. Plus, the best inflatables you can find, Johnny—Santa, Frosty, the whole crew. Oh, and make sure there's a sleigh up on the roof with reindeer—Rudolph, Vixen, all of them. . . ."

It's the day after Halloween, and Mom's already ordering Christmas.

"How was the sleepover?" she asks, all happy.

"Good." I feel sick inside. I wish I could tell her what happened last night, but then she'll know I lied about where I was staying. Well, I didn't really lie. I just didn't make it clear. . . .

"Are you okay, Mackie?" Mom walks closer, staring at my face.

"I think I might be coming down with something."

She tests my forehead with the back of her hand. "You don't feel warm."

She keeps staring at me. "Anything you want to talk about?"

I feel like I'm going to cry. "No, I'm good."

"Don't let Rory get to you," Mom says.

Why does everything have to be about Rory? I have a life too, you know.

"He still gets so jealous of you," Mom says.

What? How could that be possible? "What do you mean?"

"It was hard for Rory when you were little. Before you were born, he was the center of the universe. The first child—the first grandchild. And then you came along. And you were just the sweetest, happiest baby. Everyone adored you. Especially your Gramp." Mom laughs. "Poor Rory would romp around like a circus monkey just trying to get attention. . . ."

I can't believe my mother is saying this. I wish I had a video camera or a tape recorder or something.

"Everything okay at school?" Mom asks. "What do you have for homework?"

I tell her about the story I'm writing on Gramp.

She smiles. "That's nice."

"Hey, Mom." I hesitate. I pour some juice, trying to sound like it's no big deal. "I was wondering . . . will I ever get to meet my other gramp . . . your dad?"

"No, Mack," she says, "probably not."

"Well, can you just tell me about him? I'm not a baby any—"

"Mack, stop." Mom walks into the family room and sits down in the window seat, the one nobody ever sits in. I can't remember the last time I saw my mother just sitting, anywhere. She's always rushing around, busy. Dad, too.

Mom leans back against the cushion and looks out at the birdfeeder.

I search the cupboard for the mug I bought her last Mother's Day. The one with my face on it. I make her some tea. We have lots of these mug-shot photo-mugs, but this one is just me. Rory isn't in the picture. "Say cheese," the lady at the mall said.

Mom smiles when she sees the mug. "So handsome," she says, looking at the picture, then at me. I sit across from her in the window seat, our legs spread long, side by side.

"I'm almost as tall as you now," I say.

"You're growing up fast."

We look outside. Mom sips the tea. "It's good, Mack. Thanks."

A fat gray bird—"A mourning dove," Mom says—lands on the feeder. The squirrel on the ground looks up, hoping some seeds will fall. Mom and I sit there quiet. It's nice.

"Mack, I'm sorry." Mom's hand shakes as she sets the mug down on the windowsill. She draws her knees up to her chest and hugs her arms around them. "It's just that . . . I've worked so hard—" A cry catches in her throat. "I've worked so hard to build a new life for myself and for my children. . . ." Now she's crying.

"Mom, it's okay." I reach over and rub her arm. "Don't worry. Forget I asked about him."

A big blue jay lands and the mourning dove takes off, the feeder swings crazy and seeds scatter down. That squirrel just hit the lottery.

"You have every right to ask, Mackie. It's just, I'm not ready to remember."

"I know, Mom. It's okay."

"I love you, Mackie," she says, wiping her nose.

"I love you, too, Mom."

CHAPTER 24
WORD WORLD

KINDERGARTEN TEACHER: THE FOUR SEASONS, THE FOUR SEASONS—
SURELY SOMEONE CAN NAME THE FOUR SEASONS!
LITTLE KID NUMBER FIVE: BOWLING, KICKBALL,
HIDE-AND-SEEK, TAG?

On Monday, Mrs. Schmidt says my story about Gramp was excellent, "moving and sincere," but that next time I should "skip the thesaurus" and just use language I'm familiar with.

When I tell Mrs. Schmidt that I didn't use a thesaurus, that I know what all those words mean, she asks me if I'll take this quiz. It's not required or anything, but she is looking for a sixth grader to represent Danville Middle School at the district Word World competition. It sounds lame, but I agree to meet her during Study Hall.

The test is easy. And guess what? I've got a twelfth-grade vocabulary. I should be a senior in high school. No surprise to me.

Mom and Dad are impressed.

"He sure doesn't get it from us, Bill," Mom says. My parents are math people. They can crunch numbers and calculate taxes in their sleep, but let's just say they're not in the *New York Times* Sunday crossword-puzzle crowd.

Dad tells me to call Gram.

"Oh, Mackie, I'm so proud of you," Gram says. "I'd be happy to help you train for the competition."

"Sure, Gram, thanks. You sort of started it all with the 'fivers' thing. . . ."

Mom orders lasagna from Café Italia to celebrate. Actually, that's no big deal. We do take-out just about every night. Mom doesn't have time to cook. Dad doesn't either. They always used to fight about whose turn it was to "do dinner," and then they finally just called a truce. Everybody's a lot happier now.

Monday's Italian . . . Tuesday's Chinese . . . The Yellow Submarine when we're on the road. And, as you know by now, I make a mean mac 'n' cheese. It's all in the stirring.

I show Mom and Dad the Word World training manual. "I have to know the definition and spelling for every word, and be able to use each one in a sentence."

"Look at this, Bill," Mom says, all proud. "*Chortled.*"

Dad smiles. "It sounds familiar, but I'm not sure. What's the definition, Mack?"

"*Chortle* means 'to laugh,'" I say. Mom and Dad and I chortle.

Rory is staring at me like he's going to puke. He pokes at his food. He doesn't like it that I'm better than him at something. He's jealous.

Then Rory gets this big smile. He squints his eyes like he's trying to read something on my face. He pokes his finger in the air in my direction like he's counting.

My freckles. "Cut it out," I say.

"Wait," Rory says. "I think they spell something. Yes. Oh, my God, it's a word. L-A-M-E-R. Can you give us the definition, Mack?"

I stare at Rory, trying to think of a good comeback, and then all of a sudden I notice something. Something wonderful.

Spots.

Three big, fat red spots. One on his forehead, two on his nose.

Acne. Bingo. Happy birthday.

I squint my eyes, point my finger at Rory's face, and start counting. "One . . . two . . . three . . ."

"Shut up," he says.

"You wanted freckles, huh, Rory? You wanted to be just like me, huh?"

I chortle, and Rory shuts up.

Rory follows me upstairs after dinner. "I know where you were last night."

"So what," I say. "I know where you were too." I pucker my lips and wrap my arms around my shoulders. "Oh, Britney, Britney . . ."

Nobody's going to tell Mom *anything*.

When I finish my homework, I lie in bed thinking about Halloween. If I tell Digger it was Pope, he might fight him and get suspended. If I confront Pope, he might do something worse. That kid is twisted. He scares me.

When I close my eyes to sleep, I see Mrs. Jones's beautiful memorial, Digger's carvings smeared with blood-red paint. I hear the evil way Pope laughed, all excited, like when we were in the War Zone beneath his house. Halloween night was just another game to him. "Suckers, baiters, dominators." He was showing Digger that As dominate. He was trying to make Dig ashamed or afraid.

Pope Banker knew just what he was doing.

Now, what am I going to do?

CHAPTER 25
TRADING PLACES

Digger and I are trading places today.

I haul dirty socks and underwear out from under my bed and scrape the gum off my nightstand. I look out the window. Now that the leaves are all down, I can see across the creek to Digger's woods. Eagle House, Cardinal House, Goldfinch, Blue Jay. The memorial pole is a blood-red reminder of what happened on Halloween night.

Coming home from school, I sit in Digger's usual spot on the back of the bus. Digger stayed after for my soccer game. Coach has to play him in my position. Ms. O-B wants each of us to truly experience a typical day in our neighbor's moccasins—or, in this case, cleats. Angel Nelson gives me a piece of grape bubblegum. She's trading places with Diva Landerly and ought to be sitting up front next to Whitney Reed, but Diva said no way was she sitting in the C section.

Nigel, Taylor, Angel, and I talk about the Danville Day soccer tournament. Six teams have entered. Bart Schufelt's been bragging about the Brentwood team he put together. His father hired a pro to coach.

When I told Rory about Mr. Jones's team, he laughed. "You're playing with *girls*?" Rory laughed about it all night, and then the next day he went out and put together an Avalon team for the tournament. Andy Slater, Matt Gleason, Bruce Faddegon, Britney Scooter, Whitney, Diva Landerly . . .

I think Rory just wants more face time with Britney. He's spending a lot of time with her. He hasn't mentioned the Freebirds in weeks. I wonder if he still wants to go.

When the bus stops at Digger's house, Pope Banker sniffs at me as I get off. "Where are you going, Flack?"

"Homework," I say.

Sunshine runs out to welcome me. She has her daisy sneakers on. "Come on, Mack," she says, taking me by the hand.

It's cold in the house. Mr. Jones smiles. "Welcome home, son."

"Hi, Dad," I say, and we laugh.

"I'm off to work. Plenty in the fridge for dinner. Sunshine's bedtime is eight o'clock. All set?"

"Don't worry," I say.

Mr. Jones gives me the emergency number at the meat-packing plant. He doesn't have a cell phone. He scoops

Sunshine up for a hug and then swipes the top of my head. "Call me if you need me, Mack. I'll try not to wake you when I get home."

"Okay," I say. "No problem."

It's freezing in here. Mom keeps our house at seventy-four degrees. I look for a thermostat, and then I remember. They burn wood for heat.

"Don't forget to open it," Sunshine says, pointing up at the fireplace flue. *Flue* is in the Word World manual. Mrs. Schmidt says it's the little words that'll get you. Some kids skip right over the three- and four-letter words and just study the big guys. Last year, the contestant from DMS got eliminated in the very first round on the word *mutt*. She forgot the second *t*. That must have hurt.

I open the flue so the smoke will go up the chimney. I lay down some sticks for kindling, strike a match, and light the ends. When the fire catches, I pile on some logs, crisscrossing them to let the air circulate, the way Digger taught me.

"Want a snack?" Sunshine asks. We go into the kitchen.

Sunshine puts out an oatmeal cookie for each of us. I pour us some milk. "Digger made them last night," she says. "What are you cooking us for dinner, Mack?"

"Something good," I say. I try not to stare at her eye patch.

I open the refrigerator. No take-out cartons. No deli meat.

I open the freezer. No frozen dinners. No leftover pizza. There are bags marked "chili" and "venison stew" with expiration dates. This could be trouble. Sunshine looks worried.

I open the cupboard. *Happy birthday*. There are two beautiful blue boxes of mac 'n' cheese calling out my name. "Sweet."

Sunshine laughs. "Digger got them for you. He said that's what you'd make."

We sit at the table by the fire. Sunshine draws pictures and colors them while I do homework. Every once and a while, she looks over, but she doesn't bother me. When I finish, I look at her pictures. A lady with long black hair sitting on a cloud dropping daisy petals down to a girl. A girl with a patch on her eye riding on a turtle's back . . .

"These are beautiful, Sunshine. You're a really good artist."

"I miss her," Sunshine says, still coloring. "I wish I could be with her."

I'm not sure what to say. "But what about your dad and Digger? They'd miss you."

"I know," Sunshine says, shrugging her shoulders like she's sorry, but they would just have to deal with it.

"And what about Go, Sunshine? Who'd take care of him?"

"Maybe Go would be happier down in the Creek. . . ."

"No, Sunshine, it's too cold. He'd rather stay here with you."

The phone rings. Mr. Jones checking on us. Sunshine says she's hungry.

"Chef McGinn reporting for duty," I say with a salute. Sunshine laughs and we head into the kitchen. She sets out spoons and bowls while I make my specialty.

"It's good, Mack," Sunshine says, shoveling the cheesy noodles into her mouth. "Digger said you'd do a good job."

We finish our bowls and I scoop us some more. I probably should have put out bread or carrots or grapes or something to go with it, but Sunshine and I don't care. After dinner, we eat more oatmeal cookies. There isn't a dishwasher. This could be trouble.

Sunshine puts a plug in the sink and turns the faucet on. She squirts in the soap. I wash and rinse. Sunshine dries. She gives Go some lettuce and bread. I wipe off the table. Sunshine goes to get her pajamas on. So far, so good.

I wonder how Digger's doing? I hope Mom's being nice to him.

"Read to me, Mack," Sunshine says, patting the spot next to her. There's a stack of books on the nightstand. "This first," she says.

"A Chair for My Mother," I read, "by Vera B. Williams."

"See her," Sunshine says, smiling, pointing to the girl with long black pigtails on the first page. "And, look, that's her mom."

The girl's mother is a waitress. They don't have much money. The girl wants to buy a chair for her mom to relax in when she comes home from a hard day's work.

"Point to the words," Sunshine tells me. She knows the story by heart. When we get to the last page, Sunshine pats the girl, fast asleep in her mother's arms.

We read three more books. Finally, Sunshine yawns.

"Good night," I say. "Sleep tight. Don't let the bed bugs bite."

"Wait, Mack." Sunshine reaches for my hand. "We have to thank the Creator."

Q. WHY WAS THE BASKETBALL PLAYER SENT TO JAIL?
A. FOR SHOOTING BASKETS AND STEALING BALLS.

Rrrrrrrrrr, blumph, blumph, blumph, Rrrrrrrrrrrrrrrrrrrrrrrr-rrrrrrrrrrrrrr . . .

It's Saturday morning, but who can sleep with that army of machines roaring outside. They are roaming every inch of Avalon, smoking every last leaf from its hole.

General Mom is down front with Mr. Nelson. Angel and her dog aren't in the truck today. It's not even Thanksgiving yet, but Mom is overseeing the installation of Christmas. It will be hard to beat Halloween, but the General's on top of this mission.

There are huge inflatable holiday floats all over our front lawn. Frosty the Snowman's face bops by my window. Garfield, the Grinch, Sponge-Bob Square Pants. Penguins skate around inside a giant snow globe. Up on the roof, a row of mechanical Rockettes kick it up good next to Rudolph and the gang. *Choo-chooo, choo-choo, chug-a-luga-luga-lug, chug-a-luga-luga-lug* . . . A train full of presents chugs around the property. "All aboard," the plastic conductor shouts.

And towering above it all is the big dude himself, a King Kong–size Santa Claus, waving, winking, laughing, singing. "I'm making a list and checking it twice, gonna find out who's naughty . . ." There are thousands, no, millions of lights.

An old station wagon pulls into the Bankers' circle. The royal cats' birthday bash is tonight. A guy in a long brown robe gets out. He's wearing sandals like it's summertime. Then a lady gets out, dressed head to toe in blue. She looks like Our Lady of Perpetual Sorrows. She's holding a baby wrapped in a blanket. *Weird.*

I dress and bike up to the park. There's frost on the fields. My ears are cold. My nose is running. I wish I wore gloves. I stretch, check the clock, and run.

Breathe in and out and run. *Chh . . . run, run, run. Chh . . . run, run, run.* There's the Golden Turkey gobbling fast before me. *Chh . . . run, run, run. Chh . . . fast, fast, fast. Chh . . . win, win, win, faster, faster.* I think about Rory calling me at the Roadrunner race. "Mackie, Mackie." Next Saturday, I won't be so stupid. On Danville Day, at the Turkey Trot, I'll blow this whole town away. I'll run like a cyclone. The crowd will be roaring, "Mack-ie, Mack-ie . . ." Dad crying so proud. Cameras flashing. "Cheese." Mack McGinn's big win.

* * *

"Your friend Digger is quite a soccer player," Dad says to me at breakfast. "He scored two goals against Shaker for you yesterday. He should have made the DMS team. I told Coach Barnes that. And that kid can cook, too. Meatloaf from scratch, mashed potatoes and carrots—he steamed them, I think—and apple cobbler for dessert."

"Yeah," I say. "Dig's going to be a chef someday."

Mom follows me upstairs. "Can I talk to you?" she says.

Mom and Digger had a heart-to-heart last night. Digger explained the whole story of how Sunshine lost her eye. I thought I was the only person who knew. He swore me to secrecy when we were blood brothers.

It happened right before Thanksgiving, a few months after Mrs. Jones died. Mr. Jones had promised Digger all year that he would take him hunting. It was a really big deal for Dig. He and his dad would take home a deer, enough to keep the freezer stocked with venison for the winter.

Sunshine put up a tantrum and begged to go. She wouldn't stay with a neighbor or babysitter. After her mother died, Sunshine clung to Digger, couldn't bear to see him leave for school. And so all three of them bundled up and headed for the mountains.

They pitched a tent by a small lake in the Adirondacks. Digger helped his father cook dinner on the grill. Afterward, Mr. Jones headed off to sleep. Digger told stories to Sunshine and then tucked her into her sleeping bag. The fire was still burning strong, so Dig decided to roast some marshmallows. One got too close to the flames and started burning. Dig was blowing out the flames when he heard something behind him and turned quickly. Too quickly. Too close to Sunshine's face. Too close to Sunshine's beautiful brown eye.

"That poor girl," Mom says, shaking her head. "And that poor boy, Digger, having to live with that awful memory every day." Mom starts to cry. "I had no idea. . . ."

I think about saying, no, you didn't, Mom. You judged Dig without knowing the truth. Just like you blamed him for the water-balloon war when it was Pope . . . But I can see my Mom feels bad enough. I hug her, and she cries harder.

There's one other part of the story you should know.

As they waited outside the emergency room that morning while the doctors took care of Sunshine, Mr. Jones told Digger, "It was an accident, son." He took Digger's face in his hands and said, "Listen to me. It wasn't your fault. It was a tragic accident and it's over. I don't ever want you to blame your-self."

CHAPTER 27
THE ROYAL CATS'
BIRTHDAY BASH

Q. WHAT DID THE REF CALL WHEN THE PLAYER THREW A PIG IN THE END ZONE? A. ILLEGAL USE OF HAMS.

At seven o'clock we leave for the Royal Cats' Birthday Bash. We are dressed like we're going to Buckingham Palace. Buddy barks, wishing he could come.

Mom gives Bud a treat and pats his head. She's feeling especially happy tonight.

"I can't wait to see the Bankers' live nativity," Mom says. "Goldie held auditions this morning. They've got Mary and Joseph and the baby Jesus, the little drummer boy, shepherds, angels, all the animals . . ."

Bud barks hopefully.

"Forget it, Bud," I say. "You're a dog, not a cow."

Mom stops on the sidewalk out front of our house. "Turn around and look," she says, her face all bright in the holiday lights. "Isn't it spectacular?"

"Yeah, Mom," I say. "You won for sure."

"It's not a competition, Mack."

"Yeah, right."

"Look," Rory says, "people on horses."

We turn and watch them coming up the street. Three men, dressed in capes and wearing crowns. And they aren't riding horses. They're riding camels.

"Holy sh--," Rory says.

"Don't swear," Dad says.

"It's the three kings," Mom says.

The kings process by and we join the parade, careful not to step on camel crap.

The Bankers beat us for sure.

At the manger, the baby Jesus starts crying. Mary sticks a bottle in his mouth. The sheep *baaa*. The cows *moo*. I see the wires that will keep them from leaving.

We ring the doorbell. The butler answers and hands us pink party hats. You can tell the guy feels really stupid doing this.

"No way," Rory says.

"Just wear them," Mom pleads. She owes us big-time for this.

"Jeannie, Bill." Goldie Banker swoops toward us in a gold gown. "Poper!" she yells. "The boys are here!"

Poper? Oh, that's rich.

Goldie smiles at me and Rory. "The food is that way, boys. The carving station just opened."

Goldie's Girls—Fur, Her, Myrrh, Purr, and Sir—are perched in their royal chairs around the dining room table. Goldie rings a bell and five men in tuxedos file in, each carrying a silver tray. One man stands at attention behind each cat. Goldie rings again and the men whisk the tops off the platters and lay them down. "Fresh grilled tuna with mango chutney," the men say in chorus, like they practiced.

"Poper" is showing Rory the War Zone. I don't see anybody else I know. It's all grown-ups. I don't think Poper has any friends. I carefully lift a china plate from the stack and head for the "carving station."

"Turkey, ham, or beef?" the chef asks.

"All three, please. Load me up."

The long table is covered with food. I pile on three different kinds of potatoes and two pastas, Alfredo and marinara, and sit down in the corner to eat. When the pantry door swings open, I see bakers putting finishing touches on the royal cats' birthday dessert. Five identical pink fish-shaped cakes. I hope they've got people cake too.

I'm bored. I go get more food. I hear Goldie and Mom talking.

"They're my baby girls, Jeannie," Goldie says, smiling, stroking Fur and then Myrrh. Or maybe Her and then Sir. Who knows—they all look alike. Goldie shakes her head, all of a sudden looking tragically sad. "You can't imagine how hard it's been, Jeannie, all these years, not having a daughter. No one to shop with. No one to spa with . . ." She starts to cry.

I'm going to puke, and not just because I ate too much. I want to get out of here. I go to look for Dad.

He's in the living room with Plat Banker. Plat is handing Dad a cigar. Dad doesn't smoke, but he takes it anyway, probably just to be nice.

"Have you seen that dump across the creek?" Plat says, sucking in on the cigar to get it going. He nods toward his wall-to-wall, floor-to-ceiling window. It's like the size of the window in the airport where you can look out and see the planes. I've never seen such a big window in a house.

"Those shacks have got to go," Plat says, blowing out a big cloud of smoke. "I didn't spend two million dollars to look out my back window and see a slum . . ."

My heart is pounding; my ears are hot. He's talking about Digger's woods.

". . . pagan tree forts and . . . a telephone pole they painted red . . ."

My stomach feels punched. *Your son did that, you a-hole. That's a sacred memorial pole. It was beautiful. Digger carved it himself after his mother was killed in the war. A real war. Not the make-believe, whacked-out kind you do in your basement . . .*

"I called the town," Plat says, sucking on his cigar again, puffing smoke in Dad's face. He takes a long sip of his drink and nearly breaks the glass when he slams it down. "Danville won't do anything. They say it's private property. Bunch of sissy-ass skirts. But I say, that ghetto's going. That red pole's coming down first. We have to preserve our views, McGinn. Right? If we don't, our property values'll go down the shitter. Are you with me on this, or what?"

Another punch in my gut, deeper, harder. I feel hot and cold and scared.

Then something in me snaps. I move toward them. My legs are shaking. Dad looks up and sees me. Then Plat Banker does. "Come on in, son," he says, all nice, smiling. "Your father and I were just talking about . . ."

"Pope did it," I say, my heart pounding so hard I can hear it. "He vandalized the Joneses' property on Halloween night. He desecrated a sacred burial site and . . ."

CHAPTER 28
THE BEST
THINGS IN LIFE

**Q. WHAT DO YOU CALL A PLAYER WHO
FALLS ASLEEP IN THE BULLPEN?
A. A BULLDOZER**

Right after my little speech, we left the Royal Cats' Birthday Bash in a flash. Rory had just come back up from the War Zone. Dad grabbed Mom's arm and said, "We're going."

"Oh, no," Goldie protested, pouting like a baby. "The Girls are just about to open their presents." She winked at me and Rory. "And we have goodie bags!"

"*Now*, Jean," Dad insisted, yanking the pink hat off his head and throwing it on the marble floor.

We're sitting at our kitchen table. At first Mom was mad about leaving the party, but now she's disgusted when she hears what Pope did to Digger on Halloween night. "How violent . . . hateful. Just despicable."

"Why didn't you tell us, Mack?" Dad says. Rory's lost in the refrigerator, looking for food. He never made it to the carving station.

I explain that I was afraid to tell them where I was on

Halloween night because I knew they didn't want me at Digger's house.

"I thought you were with your soccer team from school," Dad says.

"I thought you were here in Avalon," Mom says.

Mom and Dad look at each other. Dad shakes his head. Mom sighs. "We need to ask better questions, Bill."

Rory slams the refrigerator door. Bud barks. "That kid's evil," Rory says, "twisted. When he took me down in the elevator, at first I was like, *sweet*, a pool hall, an arsenal—"

"An *arsenal*?" Mom eyes bug out.

"And the War Zone is awesome," Rory says.

"What do you mean, a *war zone*?" Mom's voice is shaky.

"It's what they call their laser tag arena," Rory says. "Pope said it cost fifty grand."

"They've got a laser tag arena in the basement?" Dad says.

"Yeah," I say. "Right under the security bunker where Pope and his father spy on the neighbors with surveillance equipment."

"*What!*" Mom is horrified.

"The War Zone was fun at first," Rory says, taking another bite of cold pizza, "but then Poper went psycho. It was like he thought he was in a real war. He came after me with his gun—"

"*Gun!*" Mom shrieks.

"Not a real one," Rory says, "but laser tag is supposed to be a noncontact sport. . . ."

"Laser tag isn't a sport," Dad says.

"It's late," Mom says, sighing loudly. "Let's go to bed."

Later, when I come back upstairs from getting a snack, I hear Mom and Dad talking. Their door is open a crack.

"I had no idea that boy was such a problem," Mom says. "No wonder he keeps changing schools. I'm surprised he's not in reform school. He sounds dangerous. And here all this time I've been pushing Mackie to play with him."

"The apple didn't fall far," Dad says. "The father's a sicko too."

Mom shakes her head. "What are we going to do, Bill?"

"There's not much we can," Dad says. "They're our neighbors."

"Oh, my god," Mom says. "I wish I'd found out more about that family before we built right next to them. I was so thrilled to get the lot, one of the last buildable lots in Avalon, and the market was prime to sell the house in Brentwood, but obviously I rushed us into . . ."

"It's not your fault, Jean. How could we have known?"

"We could have talked to some people, Bill. We spent months researching granite countertops and chandeliers and Chilean parquet."

"It's a beautiful house, Jean. It's a beautiful neighbor-hood."

"I know, but we should have been more concerned about the people our sons would be growing up, hanging out with—not the houses, *the people* in the houses. I can't believe I've been so shallow, so irresponsible . . ."

"Come here," Dad says. He wraps Mom in his arms. "You were just trying to do the best for our family. I'm proud of my real-estate maverick wife. Getting us a house in the best neighborhood in Danville. You and I both are working hard as we can to give Rory and Mack the best things in life. . . ."

Mom makes a wincing sound. She starts to cry and mumbles something.

"What?" Dad says.

"The best things in life aren't things."

"That's nice," Dad says. "Where'd you hear that? It sounds familiar."

"Don't you remember, Bill? Your father. At the Cape house. That little plaque he hung inside the front door. 'The best things in life aren't things.'"

CHAPTER 29
MACK'S SECRET

Danville Day is Saturday.

The turkey piñata arrived yesterday, and it's being filled with candy. Tons and tons and tons of candy.

"Hey, Mom," I say, "in honor of the bicentennial, how about you add some lottery tickets in with the candy. You know, to pump up the stakes a bit."

"I don't think the chamber would approve of lottery tickets for kids," Mom says.

"Well, then, how about fivers?"

"Fivers?" Mom looks confused. "What's a fiver?"

"It's a five-dollar bill all folded up tight. Gram is really good at making them."

Mom laughs. She brushes hair away from my eyes. "Sure, Mack. Why not?"

Mom gets some crisp new Lincolns from the bank and we stop by Gram's apartment. Gram says she'll be happy to turn them into fivers.

I can't remember how many of those little money squares Gram has snuck into my hands over the years, but I have a twelfth-grade vocabulary to prove it. And Gram is so happy to be my coach for the Word World competition next month. We're up to the six-letter words now.

There's a DMS soccer game after school. I score. *Sweet.* We win, four-zip. We are still undefeated for the season. Rory will definitely get MVP, but right now I'm the number two scorer. Pretty decent for a sixth grader.

Our Danville Day rec team is looking good too. We haven't had many practices because of Mr. Jones's work schedule, but when we do get together, we're strong. Digger and I are "left wing-right wing, rule," just like the old days.

On Thursday morning I head out early to the park for one last trial before the Turkey Trot on Saturday. Rory's coming down the hall to the bathroom when I leave. He looks at me, but he doesn't say anything. Rory isn't on my case so much anymore.

Lately, he's more concerned with acne medicine and hair gel and the best-smelling body spray. He showers every morning now, sometimes twice on the weekends, and brushes his teeth without General Mom even having to check.

Danville Park is empty. I hit the kickstand on my bike, but

instead of stretching out like usual, I head toward the center square.

I look up at the statue. "Hi, Gramp."

The sculptor did a good job. That's my Gramp's face, all right.

"Hey, Mack."

I swing around and there's Digger.

"What are you doing here?" I say.

"Same thing you are." He laughs. "Checking the course for the Turkey Trot, right?"

"Yeah, right."

Digger nods at the statue. "You must be pretty proud," he says. "Your gramp was some athlete. And he did a lot for Danville. He started the rec soccer program, right? And the new playground. And wasn't he the one who came up with the Turkey Trot race and the piñata and . . ."

"Yeah," I say. "My gramp was great." I turn away, tears stinging my eyes.

"Sorry, man," Dig says.

"It's okay." I pick up a gum wrapper and toss it in the trash can.

"You know, Dig, I've been running here nearly every morning since September, but I never come over to Gramp's statue . . ."

"That doesn't mean anything," Digger says.

"Yeah, Dig, it does." I kick the bench. I'm ashamed, but I don't say why.

"That's all right, Mack. I pass by Mom's memorial all the time, and sometimes I don't even . . ."

"You don't understand, Dig." And then, all of a sudden, I blurt it out.

"The night my gramp died, I was the only one, *the only one*, who didn't have the guts to say good-bye."

Digger doesn't say anything.

My voice rises. "When Dad said it was near the end, I went down to the hospital cafeteria and bought an orange soda—" My words crack in my throat. "A friggin' orange soda, and I sat there, hiding like a baby in that stupid, smelly cafeteria. . . ." I start crying. Dig looks away.

"And when I finally got the courage to go back up, Gramp was already . . ." I slump down on the bench and huddle over, my fists clenched over my eyes.

Digger sits next to me. He puts his hand on my shoulder, then drops it.

"I should have gone in there, Dig." My whole body is shaking. "My Gramp was always there for me, *always*. Every birthday. Every game. But I wasn't there for him when he needed me." Tears are running down my face. "I should have said good-bye. I should have told him I loved . . ."

"You did, Mackie." Digger stands up. "You did, man. I remember when you lived by me, every time your gramp came, you'd hug him. And you were always building those boats. I'd want to shoot hoops or something and you'd say, "No, my Gramp's here." I remember. Not everybody wants to hang out with their relatives. Your parents make you, or you do it because you feel guilty. But not you, Mack. You and your gramp were tight. I used to be jealous seeing you two sitting on your front step talking like you were best friends. That was real, Mack. And when you love somebody that strong, you're always together, no matter what. You were there with your gramp, Mack. You were there, for sure."

I hunch over and cry like a baby. I don't even try to hide it. Digger doesn't say anything else. We're still the only ones in the park.

After a while, I stand up. I wipe my nose on my sleeve. "Thanks, Dig." I look at him. "I never told anybody about hiding in the cafeteria. . . ."

"That's okay, man. Your secret's safe with me." Digger punches my chest, joking. Then he looks me straight in the eyes. "We're even now, right?"

I know what he means. "Right."

"Good," Digger says, fixing his red bandana. "Because I'm gonna whup your freckled butt on Saturday."

He races off down the trail, laughing, black hair whipping in the wind.

CHAPTER 30
DANVILLE DAY

**Q. WHY DID THE RUNNER WEAR RIPPLED-SOLE SNEAKERS?
A. TO GIVE THE ANTS A CHANCE.**

I'm dreaming of wonderful things. Bacon and sausage and cinnamon rolls. I open my eyes and sniff. I leap out of bed. It's for real. It's been a long time since anybody cooked breakfast around here, but I'm not complaining.

Downstairs in the kitchen, Dad is pouring batter on the griddle. Mom is scrambling eggs. The oven light is on. Cinnamon rolls. *Sweet.*

Rory trudges in yawning, wiping his eyes.

"Thought you boys could use some extra fuel today," Dad says.

He's talking about the Turkey Trot.

"Oh, and there's mail for you on the table, Rory." Dad looks all excited.

Rory picks up the envelope. "Freebirds," he says. He looks at Dad.

We all stare at Rory as he opens it, unfolds the letter, and reads. I can't tell by his face whether he's happy or sad. It's funny, I thought I'd be really happy if Rory moved away, but now I kind of . . .

"Well?" Dad asks, all anxious.

"I got accepted."

"All right!" Dad says, pumping his fist in the air. His eyes are wet with tears. "Congratulations, son." He rushes over to give Rory a hug.

Rory looks sort of dazed, like he's not sure what to think.

"Congratulations, Roar," Mom says. "That's quite an honor."

I nod my head. "Nice job, Roar."

Rory reads the letter again. Dad asks to see it, his face all proud. Rory sits down and pours a glass of juice.

"You don't seem excited," Dad says.

"Yeah, I am," Rory says. But it doesn't sound that way.

Mom is watching Rory. "Well, it's certainly an honor to be invited," she says. "But this is a big decision. A family decision. There are many things to consider. . . ."

I go to feed Bud. He's not in the Budroom.

"It's such a nice day," Dad says, "I let him stay out in the yard after our walk."

"But we're not fenced in yet," I say.

"Bud's not going anywhere," Mom says, laughing. "He's having a ball chasing the holiday train around the house. But I do think he's afraid of Garfield."

* * *

The Danville Day parade kicks off at nine o'clock. Blue sky, sun shining, cool, no wind. Perfect running weather.

Dad and Rory and I find a spot on the sidewalk. Mom waves to us from the lead float, followed by the Danville High marching band. Girl Scouts, Boy Scouts, dancers, clowns, men in funny hats driving funny little cars. Fire engines, jugglers, politicians. We salute the veterans as they walk by.

I remember every Fourth of July and Danville Day, Gramp would salute the veterans with such gratitude. His baseball-mitt-size hand slanted stiff against his forehead beneath that mop of white hair, chin up, chest out, his blue eyes glistening, never moving a muscle, never looking away, until every last soldier walked by.

I try to stand proud, like Gramp did.

The final float is the turkey piñata. All the kids cheer loud.

"Oh, yeah," Rory says, "I'll be whacking that bird soon."

"The winner gets first crack," I say.

Rory laughs. "Feeling confident, are you, freckle-face?"

"Yeah, I am, pimple-face. Oh, wait, Rory, look." I point across the street. "It's Britney." I pucker my lips and make kissing sounds.

Rory looks, but she's not there.

"Sucker," I say.

"Lamer," he says.

When I look back at Rory, he's smiling.

You know, I can't believe I'm saying this, but I'd miss Rory if he went to Florida.

We line up for the Turkey Trot. The starting gun will pop at eleven.

"Hey, Mack," Digger calls over to me. "Good luck."

"You, too, Dig."

Digger's fast. I remember how he nearly beat me in the Roadrunner. But I've been training on this course since September. In running, training is everything. Well, that, and focus. If your head isn't in it, you're dead.

There are lots of runners from DMS. Nobody from Avalon, though. Pope Banker hasn't been in school. I haven't had to face him since the Royal Cats' Birthday Bash.

I don't see Rory. Angel Nelson is a few rows behind. She waves, and I wave back. Maggie Carroll and her parents are sitting on a bench. Her parents look sad, as usual. Maggie's waving a flag. When she sees me, she shouts, "Good luck, Mack Mack McGinn."

"Mack-aroon!" Mom calls. Gram blows me a kiss. I've got my whole fan club here, except . . . where's Dad?

I close my eyes and take a deep breath. *Shake it off, Mackie.*

Shake it off. Eyes on the prize, Mackie. Eyes on the prize. That Golden Turkey. First.

"Ladies and gentlemen," Mayor Wilson barks through a megaphone. "Welcome to the bicentennial . . ."

I stretch my hams and quads again.

". . . a 3.2 mile, 5K road race, straight up Northern Boulevard to the reservoir, around by the town recreational fields . . ."

I roll my neck, my shoulders . . . shake out my arms . . .

Rory runs up and takes a spot three down from me in the front row. The kid he bumps is too surprised to protest. *Focus, Mackie, focus.*

"Positions!" The mayor raises the starting gun.

The crowd settles.

A ripple of energy, like electricity, sizzles through the pack.

I breathe deep. *This is it, Mack.*

"Ready . . ."

All quiet.

"Set."

POP.

I leap forward, eyes on the prize.

Phhh . . . run, run, run.

Phhh . . . fast, fast, fast.

Strong and lean and fast.

Heart . . . drum, drum, drum.

Run, run, run, run.

I'm passing bodies so fast, they're a blur. . . .

Then I hear barking. *Ruff-ruff-ruff-ruff . . .*

Sounds like Buddy.

No, it can't be. *Focus, Mack.*

Ruff-ruff-ruff-ruff-RUFF . . .

It *is* Buddy. Oh, no, what's he doing here?

Don't look, Mackie, eyes on the prize, the Golden Turkey, every second counts . . .

Ruff-ruff-ruff-ruff-ruff-ruff-ruff-ruff!

Buddy's running beside me now. He bangs against my leg. His fur is wet. He's trying to trip me. Something's wrong.

I look down, and that's when I see it.

A sneaker dangling from Bud's mouth.

A sneaker with daisies on it.

CHAPTER 31
MACK MCGINN'S
BIG WIN

Q. WHEN YOU'RE LOSING, WHAT CAN YOU COUNT ON?
A. YOUR FINGERS.

Sunshine. Oh, no. "Where is she, Bud?"

Bud bolts and I bolt after him. I look quick to see if Digger's near, but there's no time to find him. Something tells me something awful has happened.

Bud's heading toward home. I wish I had my bike. I run, *faster, faster, faster, faster.* I cross Northern without looking; a car swerves, tires screeching. The driver blares his horn. I picture Sunshine dancing in the street, cars whizzing past. *Oh, please, be inside. Please be okay.*

Chh . . . fast, fast, fast. Run, fast, fast, fast.

Bud loops back to me. He barks like *Come on, Mack, faster, faster.*

We pass the Mobil and Stewart's and Cumberland Farms. We're still two miles from home. My chest aches. My legs ache. Bud drops the sneaker. I pick it up.

Be safe, Sunshine. Be safe.

I think of the pictures she was drawing that night Dig and

I did "Trading Places." The black-haired lady and the girl. A chill creeps over my blazing hot body.

Faster, faster, faster, faster. My legs are burning. I need water.

Chh . . . run, run, run.

Chh . . . run, run, run.

Just one more mile, *come on.*

We turn into Crestwood. There's Digger's house. Thank God, Sunshine's not in the street. Bud runs through their yard past the garden and out to the woods behind. I stumble on a root; my knee slams hard on a rock. It hurts so bad, I feel dizzy. I get up and hurry down the trail. "Sunshine! Sunshine!"

When I get to the creek, I stop, my chest heaving. At first I don't see Buddy. Then, there he is, in the water, swimming toward the beaver dam. "Sunshine!" Nothing. Bud bites a stick off the dam and hurls it. Then another and another. He sticks his face in the water. Swims back to the bank and leaps up. He shakes and bolts off down the path. I follow, running again.

"Sunshine! It's me, Mackie."

The water is rushing. I chase Buddy to the drainage tunnel. He jumps back in the water. He swims into the tunnel and out again, barking like crazy at me.

"Sunshine! Sunshine!"

I can't go into that tunnel. Nothing that goes in there ever comes out alive.

When we were little, Rory showed me the giant lizard tracks on the creek bank. Slimy, sewer-fed mutant lizards. Their tongues hold your body captive while they slowly eat your face. "First your ears," Rory said, "then your nose . . ."

Grow up, Mackie. Stop it. My heart is pounding. I step into the water. It's freezing. I call into the tunnel, "Sunshine!" It's dark in there. "Sunshine!" Something bumps against my ankle in the water. "Sunshine!" My voices echoes. *Sunshine, Sunshine . . .*

The tunnel is dark and cold and scary. A channel of water runs down the center, a narrow bank of dirt on either side. I climb up onto one bank, but the ceiling's too low for me to walk upright. I crawl along in the slimy muck. There's a shape lying ahead of me.

Sunshine. She's not moving.

"Sunshine." I shake her.

I can't see her face, it's so dark. I take her in my arms. Her clothes are soaked. "Sunshine, come on. It's me, Mack." Nothing.

"Sunshine, wake up."

She doesn't move, doesn't speak, doesn't open her eyes. I hug her to my chest and haul her out of the tunnel. Her body's light and limp as a rag doll. Out in the sunlight, I see her face is gray, her lips, blue. I check for a pulse. I'm not sure. I put my cheek to her nose. Thank God, she's still breathing.

"Sunshine!"

Her eye patch has slipped. I fix it. I start to cry.

And then I run, faster than I ever have.

Faster than I ever have or maybe ever will.

I hold her tightly, gently, in my arms. She mumbles something.

"What, Sunshine?" I put my ear to her lips. I think she says, "Go."

I do. I go as fast as I can. Go, go, go, go, go. Running along the water, then up the trail, Bud next to us with the sneaker, like he thinks that it's important. "Good job, Buddy, good job." We get to Digger's house. I call an ambulance. "Hurry!" I shout into the phone. "It's an emergency."

Sunshine's still not talking or moving or anything. I pull a blanket off a bed and wrap her up. *Come on, where's the ambulance?*

"ASAP, Mackie," I hear Gram saying. "Always say a prayer."

Please, God, please, God, please, God, hurry.

I hug Sunshine to my heart and rock her like a baby.

Finally, I hear the sirens.

Swirling lights, Buddy barking. A medic attaches an oxygen

mask. They carry Sunshine out on a stretcher. I get in the back of the ambulance with her.

"I don't think that's a good idea," the medic says.

"I'm family," I say. "I'm staying with her."

And racing to the hospital, holding Sunshine's hand, never taking my eyes off her, I remember the summer Gramp and I were racing in that regatta from Mashpee to Martha's Vineyard. It was to raise money for cancer research. There was a thousand-dollar cash prize for first place. I kept shouting over the wind about the new bike I was going to buy when we won, and the fishing pole, and the megablaster water gun with the prize money. Gramp smiled at me, cheeks red from the sun, white hair whipping back, hands steady on the jib. *"Keep your eyes on the pride, Mack. Eyes on the pride."*

And all of a sudden I feel warm, like the sun just came out, like Gramp is right here with me.

"Attaboy, Mackie. I'm proud of you."

CHAPTER 32
"Say Cheese"

"Say cheese," another reporter says to me. Lights flash again, *click, click, click.*

We're in Sunshine's room at the hospital. The same hospital Gramp was in. But Sunshine is going to be okay.

Mr. Jones is here, and Digger. Mom and Dad, Gram, Rory, and Buddy. Dogs aren't usually allowed in, but the hospital makes exceptions for heroes.

"You saved my daughter's life," Mr. Jones says to me. "I don't know how to thank you, Mack." He hugs me. Bud barks like he's jealous.

"You, too, Buddy," Mr. Jones says. "You, too. Meat treats for you for a year. What do you like, Buddy, steak?"

We all laugh.

"I'm so proud of you, Mackie," Mom says. Gram hugs me for the hundredth time. Dad is staring at me, speechless.

"Good job, Red," Rory says. He punches my arm. "I mean it."

From what we were able to figure out, Sunshine decided it

was Go's time to go back home. She brought the old turtle down to the creek and put him in the water. The turtle stayed close to shore, but then it started heading toward the beaver dam. Sunshine got worried that the beaver might hurt Go, so she stepped out on a rock to try and grab the turtle back, and that's when she fell in.

The water was cold; it stunned her. Her light body was swept along by the current. Inside the tunnel, she got snagged on something and was able to crawl up onto the bank. It was dark and she was screaming for help, terrified and freezing. Eventually, her little body went into shock. The doctor said if I hadn't come when I did, Sunshine might have . . . Okay, enough of that. Sunshine is going to be fine.

Guess who won the Turkey Trot?

If you guessed Digger, *bingo*. Dig got the Golden Turkey and first crack at the piñata, felt the candy raining down on his face. Mom said the fivers were a big hit. Everyone wondered where I was.

"Look who's famous," Dad says when I come down to breakfast next morning. He holds out the Danville *Gazette*.

There I am on the front page. The headline reads DANVILLE DAY WINNER.

"You and Rory are always in the sports section," Dad says, "but you're the first one to make the news."

I pick up the paper and start reading the story.

Dad grabs my arm. His eyes are filled with tears. "I'm proud of you, Mack, really proud. I've never been more proud in my life."

"Thanks, Dad," I say. "I'm proud too. But I still sort of wish I'd won that race. . . ."

Dad grabs my arm tighter. "You did win, Mack." And then he bursts into tears and hugs me. "You won, son. You won big."

Okay, you're probably thinking the story is over. Happy ending, see ya later.

But, no, there's one more thing.

The Danville Day Rec Soccer Tournament had to be rescheduled because Mr. Jones was in charge of it, and as you know, he and Digger got called away to the hospital for Sunshine right after the Turkey Trot.

The tournament went off on Thanksgiving morning. Rory's Avalon team folded when half the kids said it was too cold to play. Bart Schufelt begged Rory to join the Brentwood team, but Rory said no thanks. "I want to play with my brother."

I checked with Digger and Angel and everybody. They said it

would be okay, as long as Rory didn't hog the ball. Rory agreed.

Rory didn't say a word when Mr. Jones had us do deep breathing exercises. He didn't say anything when Mr. Jones reminded us we were a circle, no beginning, no end, no winner, no loser. But when Mr. Jones did the grass trick, Rory looked at me and we lost it.

In the final game of the tournament, we were tied with Brentwood for first. In the final seconds of the final quarter we were down by a point. Bart Schufelt had control of the ball and was on top of his net, with a perfect shot for the win, but Rory battled it away from him and called over, "Mackie! Mackie!"

Rory passed it to me and I took off like a bullet, dribbling down the field like my cleats were on fire, the fastest kid on the team. The fastest McGinn. Winning runs in the family.

A Brentwood defender stole the ball away from me, but only for a second. Rory got it back, and screamed, "Mackie!" Rory looked at me with this huge smile, then he kicked the ball high, right to me. And just as the final buzzer rang, I scored off a header. *A header.*

Rory hugged me. "We did it!"

Digger, Angel, and the whole team circled round and swooped me up in the air.

"Mack-ie. Mack-ie." My brother started the cheer.

Sweet. It felt so sweet, I almost cried.

But I didn't.

Oh, and, there's one more thing. How much do you owe me for all the fiver words? I made you a list in case you forgot.

But, you know what? Don't sweat it. I'm feeling magnanimous lately. It's one of my Word World words. Coach Gram says I'm taking home a trophy next month for sure.

Speaking of trophies, Digger tried to give me the Golden Turkey he won on Danville Day. "You would have won it, Mack, if you hadn't run off to save my sister."

"That's okay, Dig. I won something better."

Dad framed my front-page story about saving Sunshine and hung it in the Winner's Circle in the McGinn Museum.

Mom took the gate off the Budroom. Buddy's been pigging out on steak. He likes the hero's life.

Rory decided against the Freebirds. He said he didn't want to move to Florida. He didn't mention Britney Scooter, but I think she was a factor. And Rory held his ground about wanting to try hockey. Finally Dad gave in. Dad said maybe Rory's right about the buffet line. Maybe life's more fun when you sample.

Pope Banker is out of the picture. He got expelled from DMS for setting off the fire alarm again. The Bankers put the house on the market and left without saying good-bye. *Meow.*

DMS seems smaller now. Seneca House feels like home. Mrs. Schmidt wants to help me get my sports jokes published. Angel kissed me at the holiday dance.

But, best of all, I have my best friend back.

And you can't win bigger than that.

No, you can't win bigger than that.

P.S.: If I come to your school for a soccer game or track meet or something, make sure it's a mac 'n' cheese day, okay? And a steak on the side for Buddy. Thanks.

"FIVER" WORDS

Orifice

Relinquish

Gribble

Stalagmites

Stalactites

Protocol

Venison

Perpetual

Vocations

Gargantuan

Tether

Seething

Conditioned

Segregation

Chortled

Magnanimous

ACKNOWLEDGMENTS

With thanks to . . .

My son, Dylan, for Mack's name.

My son, Connor, for the giant piñata idea. My son, Chris, for answers to countless sports questions. My brother, Jerry Murtagh, for his song, "Neighbors." My nephew, Ryan Mahoney, and Shane Flattery, Mrs. Nancy Ferry, and students at C.V. Starr Intermediate School, Brewster, New York, for "It's not about the prize, it's about the pride." Maria Buhl and Margaret Garrett at the Guilderland Public Library. The West Mountain Inn, Arlington, Vermont, for "The best things in life aren't things." Teachers and coaches at The Doane Stuart School, Farnsworth Middle School, Guilderland Elementary School, and Guilderland Youth Soccer. Mack's "first readers"— Pamela Brumbaugh and students at the Elmer Avenue School, Schenectady, New York; Southgate Elementary, Loudonville, New York; Hamagrael Elementary, Delmar, New York (and to Kelsie Rappaport and Ben and Paula Fishbein for their jokes); and Greenfield Elementary, Saratoga Springs. My writing partners: Karen Beil, Nancy Castaldo, Robyn Dennis, Debbi Michiko Florence, Jennifer Groff, Liza Frenette, Lois Feister Huey, Rose Kent, Ellen Laird, Eric Luper, Helen Mesick, Heather Norman, and Kyra Teis. My editor, Alyssa Eisner-Henkin, for pulling out the heart of the story, and Courtney

Bongiolatti. My agent, Tracey Adams, for blue-ribbon counsel. My mother, Peg Spain Murtagh, for constant banner waving. My husband, Tony Paratore, and my brother-in-law, Jim Paratore, for their good-natured, brotherly competition, still strong after all these years.

And to every kid who's ever raced with a heart full of hope to the goal, the basket, the end zone, home plate, or a finish line of any kind: You are all "big winners" in my book.